Edwardo's sudden appearance after so many years could only mean trouble.

Candice backed away from Edwardo's touch. "Don't you think it's a little late to look in on me? You could have checked a few years ago."

Edwardo ignored the brush-off and took a step closer. "Can't we just leave the past in the past and start over here?"

Candice's mouth went dry as Edwardo moved even closer. She couldn't have spoken had she tried.

"Sometimes the past needs to be dealt with."

Candice glanced around Edwardo to see Jeremy walking up the path. He stuck out his hand to shake Edwardo's. "I'm Jeremy Braunfeld."

Edwardo took a quick step away from Candice, clearly annoyed by Jeremy's interruption. Jeremy didn't look too pleased either. "And I'm Edwardo Estanza, Candi's fiancé."

TISH DAVIS lives in Colorado with her husband and three young sons. When she isn't home-schooling, she is busy writing inspirational romance. *To the Extreme* was her first published novel. Tish hopes her writing will entertain, uplift, and draw her readers into a closer relationship with the Lord.

HEARTSONG PRESENTS

Books by Tish Davis
HP426—To the Extreme

Extreme
Grace

Tish Davis

Heartsong Presents

To my husband, Bradley. You are the love of my life and my best friend. Thank you for always encouraging me.

A note from the author:
I love to hear from my readers! You may correspond with me by writing:

Tish Davis
Author Relations
PO Box 719
Uhrichsville, OH 44683

ISBN 1-58660-528-3

EXTREME GRACE

Cover design by Ron Hall.

PRINTED IN THE U.S.A.

one

"How are you feeling, Claire?" Candice asked her twin sister. She chose a seat close to her sister and stared at the petite face so dear to her. Both Candice and Claire had blond hair, though Candice's was longer and straight while Claire's curled above her shoulders. They had the same dimpled cheeks and the green eyes that mirrored their every mood. Candice remembered how they often traded places, fooling everyone around them. Those days were past.

Claire patted her round tummy and gave Candice a wan smile. "I'm okay, but I sure will be glad when the morning sickness passes. And why did they name it morning sickness anyway? I'm sick morning, noon, and night." She gave a frustrated sigh. "I know Rick will be glad when the baby is born too. I'm just not my normal self."

Candice gave her sister's hand a compassionate squeeze. Though she couldn't relate to her sister's symptoms, she could commiserate with her. Over the past three years they had grown closer than they ever had been. "It'll be all right. Just keep in mind it won't last forever. Four more months isn't so long. Soon you'll have a precious baby to hold in your arms."

Claire nodded and rolled her eyes. "I know, I know. I keep telling myself the same thing." She awkwardly reached for a box on the floor and pulled out a picture.

"Do you remember this?" Claire asked, handing Candice a picture of the two of them. The shot was taken when they were about seven years old. Claire was dressed as a princess in a long fluffy pink gown and had a tinfoil crown perched on her head. Candice stood next to her wearing a Peter Pan costume of green tights and a pointy cap with a feather sticking out of it. She had a bow drawn and was pointing an arrow at Claire.

"You thought you were a princess." Candice stared hard at the picture. Had it not been for the obvious difference in their costumes, she would have had a hard time telling them apart. She wondered how their mother ever knew who was Claire and who was Candi. Their differences didn't appear until high school. Candice began dressing more flamboyantly, and Claire got glasses. Their behavior also changed. Claire followed the straight and narrow path, while Candice decided to follow the path of the Prodigal Son.

Candice handed the picture back to Claire. "And you found your prince," she added with a sigh. She wasn't jealous of her sister's happiness. Claire and her husband, Rick, were perfect together. It was just that Candice was lonely. The mountains where she lived and worked often felt isolated from the real world. She didn't want Claire or anyone else to know that she was tired of being alone. She'd chosen her way of life. And keeping busy seemed to help, but it didn't take away the longing.

"Don't worry, there's someone special out there for you too. Be patient and let God work out all the details."

"Who says I need anyone?" Candice glanced at her watch. "Anyway, I'd better get going. It'll take a few hours to get back up the mountain."

Claire gave her sister a knowing look but didn't comment. Changing the subject, Claire said, "I wish you didn't have so far to drive. But at least you're not in Hollywood. Not long ago you were auditioning for movies and commercials. Now you work as ski patrol at a ski resort. You always did like to ski."

"Yes, my life is a lot different now, isn't it? If you'd told me five years ago that I would be skiing every day, I would have laughed and called you a fool." Candice reached for her coat and pulled it on. "Will you call me if there are any changes with the baby? You know I'll be here as soon as I can."

Claire nodded. "Of course I'll call, Candi, but everything will be fine. Be safe on those mountain roads. I hear a snowstorm's due this evening." She struggled to get out of her chair, but Candice waved away her actions.

"Sit, Clairissa! You don't need to walk me to the door. And yes, I'll be safe. I'm pretty used to driving in snow." With a quick peck on her sister's cheek, Candice hurried to the door. "Tell Rick 'hi' for me."

Candice strode down the walk then hopped in her all-wheel-drive Subaru. Her little car could get her through any mountain weather. It could plow through fresh snow and had great traction on the icy roads. Even on the coldest mornings, the engine started right up.

Two and a half hours later she arrived at the ski resort where she worked. The snowstorm had hit, and Candice was glad to finally be home. Driving those winding roads in a snowstorm took more attention and energy than she had at the moment.

When she'd first started working at the resort a few years ago, it didn't feel like home. In fact, nowhere felt like home. As an actress, Candice had bounced around from apartment to apartment, job to job, boyfriend to boyfriend. One day she had friends, the next day they were in bitter rivalry over a job. She thought making movies was the ultimate success, and when she was selected for a role in a movie, she believed her ship had sailed in. That was how she met her fiancé, Edwardo.

Edwardo was the first man Candice had truly loved. Normally she would play with men, soaking up their affection, spending their money, and using them to her fullest advantage.

She didn't care that men adored her. She thrived on the attention, but as soon as the next prospect came into her world, she threw out the first admirer like an old pair of sneakers. Edwardo was the only man who never let her use him. He never gave her the chance. Instead, he swept her off her feet, took heartless advantage of her affections, then brought her crashing back to earth again. His rejection still stung after three years. Never had she felt so humiliated.

Needing lots of money, Edwardo had decided that Candice's talent would be his meal ticket. So he encouraged her to try for more difficult roles that would give her greater exposure and pay her more. Unfortunately, as a new actress, Candice didn't stand a chance in that realm. At her first audition with big-name actors, she forgot her lines. Everyone laughed at her, including Edwardo. Word of the fiasco quickly spread, and Candice no longer had a place in the film industry. Of course, Edwardo had moved on to his next conquest. Candice had run home, ashamed and heartbroken.

Thankfully, Claire was there to help her pick up the pieces. She reminded Candice of their childhood faith that she had left behind for the bright lights of Hollywood. She showed her that God was still waiting for her and that He still loved her. After suffering heartache and humiliation, Candice returned to her Savior. She gave up her old way of life. She no longer wanted to be the highest paid, most popular actress. She didn't need to attend the high-profile parties. And she no longer desired to rub elbows with the biggest movie-makers of Hollywood. Those things offered her no comfort or lasting satisfaction. They were empty and vain. Candice didn't want to be empty and vain any longer.

She chose to walk away from that lifestyle because she could not separate her career from the mistakes she had made. No longer was she Candi Drakeforth, the starlet. She was once again Candice Drakeforth. She didn't turn heads on the street. She didn't demand attention. She wanted to be left alone, to figure out who she was and where she was going. She hoped to find those answers on the ski slopes of Colorado.

As a child, Candice had excelled at winter sports. She loved downhill skiing and cross country skiing. Ice skating wasn't her forte, and she avoided ice rinks. For winter vacations, the Drakeforth family always rented a cabin and enjoyed all the entertainment the mountains had to offer. Candice had fond memories of sledding, sipping hot cocoa, and building snowmen. She, Claire, and their parents held snowball fights, built snowmen, then fell in the snow and formed snow angels with their arms and legs. As an adult, Candice had decided to go back to those same mountains.

Candice wasn't really sure what she was searching for. She knew she didn't miss her old way of life with the artificial beauty and superficial friendships. Sometimes she missed Edwardo, or thought she did. But that was mostly when she was snowbound in her small apartment and feeling lonely. Her longing was small and nagging. It was intangible, yet very real to her. She couldn't identify it with a label, but she knew there was something missing in her life. Candice knew it probably had something to do with the fact that she couldn't let herself feel forgiven for all the rotten things she had done to other people. She had been selfish, stubborn, and prideful, just to name a few of her more noticeable flaws. It was difficult waking up each morning knowing there was a long list of people she had hurt. Whenever she thought of her past with Edwardo, she curled her fists in anger and closed her eyes until the ugly moment passed.

Cold wind and heavy snow blasted Candice as she stepped from her car. She rushed along the snowy path from the parking lot to the small, ground-floor apartment she shared with another girl. The apartment was much smaller than what she was accustomed to, but she didn't mind. She worked so much that she spent little time at home. As Candice breezed into the apartment, her roommate, Lindsey, called out to her.

"Hey, you're home! Come in here and meet my guests."

Candice dumped her stuff in the doorway, checked her hair in the hall mirror, then followed the voices into the living room. Several couples sat around the coffee table. Candice didn't recognize any of them so she casually waved at the group, then headed toward her room.

"Wait, Candice! Let me introduce you!" Lindsey called.

Reluctantly, Candice turned back to the group. She didn't feel like socializing. She was tired after her long drive, and the next day was a workday. All she wanted was a hot bath and her warm bed. She didn't appreciate that everyone in the room had stopped talking and was staring at her. Candice shifted uncomfortably.

Lindsey jumped up from the sofa and wrapped her arm around Candice's shoulders. "Everybody, this is my roommate, Candice." She began pointing at various guests, and Candice tried to follow the introductions.

"This is Gayle and Keith, they've been over before. And over here is Matt. And that is Matt's friend Jeremy. Jeremy is new to the mountain. This weekend will be his first time skiing. He is building luxury condos on our fine mountain."

Candice nodded and smiled politely at the guests, though their names flew from her mind as quickly as she heard them. But Jeremy snagged her gaze. Something about him seemed very familiar, and the sensation wasn't comfortable. There wasn't anything unusual about his appearance. His sandy brown hair was tousled. He had brown eyes and a lean face. He appeared to be slender as he lounged comfortably on the couch. She certainly didn't know anyone who built condos for a living. Candice dropped her gaze. She hoped Jeremy didn't remember her. However she knew him, it probably hadn't been a pleasant experience for him. He was probably another of the many people she owed an apology.

"Why don't you pour a soda and join us, Candice?"

Candice briefly met Jeremy's gaze before answering. His expression was unreadable as he stared back at her. Candice shook her head at her roommate.

"I don't think so, Lindsey. But thanks. I've had a long drive, and I'm ready for bed." Candice waved at the group. "It was nice meeting you all."

੨

As hard as Candice tried, she could not relax. After a long hot bath and a brief Scripture reading, Candice was ready to drop into bed. But as soon as her head hit the pillow, thoughts began flying through her mind. At the center of all those thoughts stood Jeremy.

She didn't even know Jeremy's last name. Nothing about his first name triggered a memory, although his face did remind her of someone. The only thing she knew was that he was connected to her past. It was an awful feeling to not remember how she knew him. He was a nice-looking man. Yet he wasn't the flashy type that used to appeal to her. His appearance was casual and understated, but he exuded confidence. She wondered if he had been one of her many male admirers whom she hadn't given a second thought to.

With an aggravated sigh, Candice punched her pillow to fluff it, then pulled her blankets under her chin. She willed her mind to stop spinning, but it wouldn't obey. Long after Lindsey's guests left and she had gone to bed, Candice tossed and turned. She wished she could remember who Jeremy was, yet she was afraid to remember. Eventually she slipped into a restless sleep only to be awakened by her alarm a few hours later.

❧

"You are so lucky," Lindsey gushed later that morning as she and Claire prepared for work.

"Why do you say that?" Candice bit into a piece of toast while she shoved her feet into snow boots.

Lindsey brushed her short brown hair away from her eyes. "You get to ski all day long, and you're partners with some of the best ski hunks I've ever seen. I get to sign up little kids for ski school. You get the prestige and respect. You're ski patrol. I get the snotty kids crying for mama all day. I wish I could trade one day with you." Lindsey sighed wistfully.

"Don't forget the broken bones and the irresponsible boundary breakers I get to deal with. When there's a blizzard, you stay nice and warm. I dream of the warmth you enjoy. I get to rescue runaway kids from your ski school. I get to haul injured people twice my size down the mountain. And I get all those wonderful drills and trainings on my day off. Sounds real glamorous, doesn't it?"

Lindsey shrugged. "I don't care what you say. You have a cool job. Everybody last night thought so too. Jeremy asked all sorts of questions about you."

Candice studied her friend. "What sort of questions?"

"He wanted to know what you used to do before you were with ski patrol. He asked if you are married and what you're like to be around. Sounds like he's really interested in you." Lindsey gave Candice a teasing wink.

Candice pulled on her coat without answering. It sounded like Jeremy remembered her too. Candice groaned. She hoped she wouldn't have to see him again. Why couldn't her past stay in the past? It was going to be a long day of dealing with her memories.

Candice hurried to work, received her instructions for the day, then hustled outside. She didn't want to feel trapped in the warm ski patrol office. She didn't feel like having a conversation with anyone yet. They wouldn't understand her sullen mood and would ask all sorts of questions she didn't want to answer. Until she could properly bury Jeremy's image, her day was going to be a challenge.

The brisk morning air greeted her as she pushed through the door. The crunchy feel of snow under her feet and the cold air in her lungs cheered her slightly. She just needed to get up the mountain and take a quick trail sweep to get her blood pumping and to clear her mind.

Candice popped each of her stiff ski boots into the bindings of her skis, then reached for her poles. Every time she snapped her feet into her skis, she felt such a sense of satisfaction. The action brought back memories of childhood ski vacations and happy times.

"Hey, Movie Queen, you ready yet?" called Craig, Candice's partner for the day. He waited for her a few yards off. He was already geared up, and he stared impatiently at Candice.

Candice tried not to roll her eyes. She didn't like being partnered with Craig, and she would be stuck with him all day. Craig's favorite picture was a mirror. His favorite topic was himself. To top it off, he didn't hold her in very high esteem. For whatever reason, she and Craig had been at odds from the first time they met. They just didn't get along.

"Coming!" Candice answered. She did one final check of her gear, then maneuvered over to where Craig waited for her near the chairlift. They chose the aisle marked for ski patrol. Their clothing set them off from the other skiers. Both wore black ski pants topped by red coats with big white crosses on the back. Each also carried a radio which was strapped into a first-aid belt that held basic supplies.

Wordlessly, Craig and Candice shuffled side by side to the designated point where they loaded onto the chairlift. Sitting down hard, Candice felt the chair swing as it moved forward, whisking her from the ground. Soon her feet dangled high above the ground. Candice reached for the safety bar above her head and pulled it down. Both she and Craig adjusted themselves for the five-minute ride up the mountain.

"Please don't call me Movie Queen anymore, Craig. You know it bothers me."

Craig smirked at Candice. "It's a part of who you are, isn't it? I saw you in all those commercials and movies. You should feel flattered I even remember."

"Look, Craig, I've given you my reasons. My life is different now. I'm not the same person, and I don't like to be reminded of those days. Can you lay off, please?"

Craig held up his hands. "I know, I know! You've become religious. You choose communion over beer and prayers over cussing. You don't have to remind me."

Candice decided to ignore Craig rather than correct him. He was so difficult, and she didn't understand why. She wasn't sure if he disliked her because she had been in movies or because she was a Christian. Perhaps it was just because she was a woman who was good at her job. She didn't know his reasons for antagonizing her, but she hoped one day it would stop. Her patience wore thin whenever she was around Craig, and she was tired of always being on her guard when she was with him.

Turning slightly in her seat, Candice stared across the snowy treetops. It was a warm day, as far as winter days go in the mountains. Not a breeze stirred. Tiny snowflakes flittered through the crisp air, sparkling in the sunlight. Candice inhaled the cold fresh air, and her breath came out in white puffs. God's creation always amazed her as she stared at the beautiful scenery. God planned each tree and each tiny snowflake. Nothing was a mistake, and nothing was done without His word.

Craig's voice broke rudely into Candice's reverie. "Wake up, Movie Queen. We're at the top."

Candice saw they were quickly approaching the point where the chairlift slowed and they would disembark. She slid her skis off the rest bar and allowed Craig to lift the safety bar above their heads. Candice held both poles in her left hand and scooted to the edge of the seat. Together, they rose from the seat and allowed the chairlift to push them down the snowy ramp. Candice skidded to a stop next to Craig and adjusted her goggles.

Craig didn't even glance at her. "Make sure your radio is on the right channel," he barked. "I don't want to have to search the channels if I need you. I'll take the three west runs, you take the east ones." Before Candice could respond, Craig took off in the opposite direction.

Candice made a face at his back, then immediately regretted her actions. Just because he wasn't a nice person didn't mean she could act so unprofessionally. Every skier on the mountain knew by her clothing that she worked for the lodge.

Candice set out for the eastern trails. She had to laugh at Craig's selection. He gave himself all the green and green-blue runs. Green runs featured flatter slopes and the trails were generally wider to make things easier for beginners. Blue runs were a little steeper for intermediate skiers. Candice was sure Craig hoped to find a damsel in distress on one of those slopes. She knew he liked to appear macho and knowledgeable to the beginners.

It was fine with Candice to be on the harder side of the mountain. She had one blue run and two black runs. The blue one, called "Skier's Bluff," was relaxing to monitor. She liked its long winding slope. The only thing she didn't like was that the last quarter of the run was shaded and became crusty in the afternoon. It was more difficult to maneuver turns on crusty snow, and many inexperienced skiers wiped out at that point.

The black runs were more difficult than the blue. The slopes were steeper and narrower. Waist-high mounds called moguls dotted the slopes, and the experienced skier had to slice around them with short, choppy turns. Candice enjoyed the challenge of moguls. She smiled at the thought of her sister, Claire. Claire hated moguls. They intimidated her, and she would never choose a slope that had them. If she got on one by accident, she took off her skis and walked down the slope until she was past the section of moguls.

Candice paused at the top of Skier's Bluff to allow some other skiers to go before her. After they were well below her on the hill, Candice leaned forward slightly. The weight shift set her skis in motion, and she began sliding down the mountain. The wind was cold and wet on her cheeks, but Candice didn't care. She loved the carefree feel of speeding down the mountain. With slight shifts of her weight she was able to make small gliding turns with her skis, controlling her speed. Only minutes later she was already halfway down the run to the point where the snow was crustier.

"Uh oh!" Candice stopped momentarily to take in the scene before her. A small group of skiers gathered around a downed skier. Normally she wouldn't pay them too much attention, but someone had driven a pair of skis into the snow, forming an "X." That meant they needed help.

Candice hurried down the slope to where the downed skier lay. He was too close to the trees, and she feared he might have gone out of control and hit one. She imagined he was another of those high-risk skiers looking for a thrill. She wished she could save them from injuries by keeping them out of the trees and on the designated trails.

"Is everyone okay?" Candice called as she skidded to a stop near the group.

One man pointed to the downed skier and said, "He was going really fast and couldn't stop. He hit one of those trees up there, then slid to this spot. His skis went one way, his poles another. You should have seen the snow flying!"

Before the witness finished his version of the accident, Candice was out of her skis and kneeling next to the injured skier. He was conscious but in obvious pain.

"Tell me where it hurts," she instructed calmly. Her voice took on a soothing quality that kept skiers from panicking.

"My shoulder," the skier gasped. "And my knee too." He leaned back in the snow. "I think I broke my whole body when I hit that tree."

Candice could see that his forehead was bleeding. She removed her first-aid belt and withdrew some gauze to bandage the cut. "Tell me your name," she instructed in order to distract him. She didn't want her movements to cause any more pain.

"My name is Jeremy." He winced when Candice pressed the sterile bandage to his head.

Candice's hand stilled at the mention of his name. *Jeremy? As in the Jeremy I met last night?* She groaned inwardly. It was a big ski resort. How did he get injured on her side of the mountain?

"Well, Jeremy, it looks like you're banged up pretty badly. I'm going to call up more help to get you off the mountain. Once you're down at the bottom, a first-aid tech will take a look at your injuries." Candice forced her voice to sound normal and professional, as though Jeremy were just another skier needing her help. She grabbed her radio and quickly gave their location. "A snowmobile is on its way up."

Jeremy grabbed her arm. "Will you stay with me? I don't want to lay here all alone until they get here."

Candice nodded, though she wished she were anywhere else.

Only a few minutes passed before the snowmobile pulling an empty toboggan roared up the ski slope. As curious onlookers watched, Candice helped move Jeremy to the bright orange toboggan. She could tell he was experiencing serious discomfort. "Hopefully it won't be too rough a ride for you, Jeremy. This toboggan is brand new with a thick soft foam to cushion you." She pulled the three sets of straps tight across Jeremy's body. "I'll be right behind you, all right, Jeremy?"

Jeremy didn't answer but kept his gaze on Candice's face. Candice gave him a gentle smile. "Don't worry about your gear. It will be taken care of. See you at the bottom."

Candice slowly followed the snowmobile down the mountain and watched the emergency crew gently unload him from the toboggan. She waited outside the first-aid station as Jeremy's injuries were checked. She could think of a thousand reasons to leave, but her feet remained grounded near the door. She didn't want to face Jeremy again, yet she knew she had to wait. As she glanced at her watch again, thinking she really didn't need to stay, a technician opened the door and poked his head outside.

"Hey, this guy in here wants to talk to you. Got a minute?"

"Is he going to be all right?" Candice asked.

"Yeah, it doesn't look like anything is broken, but he won't be on the slopes anymore today. Tough luck for him."

Candice followed the tech into the first-aid office. She found Jeremy sitting on one of the examination tables, his left arm hanging in a wide sling and a white bandage covering his forehead. His expression remained unreadable as he studied Candice.

She walked across the room, then paused a few feet away from him, uncertain how to proceed. She wasn't sure if she should mention that she recognized him or merely talk about his injuries and forget the past. Jeremy didn't give her a chance to say anything.

"I recognized you last night, but I didn't want to say anything in front of the others," he began.

Candice strained to hear his softly spoken words. She liked the rich sound of his voice, though his reminder of the past wasn't encouraging. The two first-aid techs were at the other side of the room, laughing at something. Candice glanced at them uncomfortably, then looked back at Jeremy.

Jeremy continued. "I've waited a long time to tell you these things, and now I'm not even sure how to say it. I used to lie awake nights, thinking of just what I would say when I saw you. Now I have the chance, and it won't come out as I planned."

Candice eyed him quizzically, afraid of what he might say, yet curious. "Why don't you just try to say it," she prompted.

Jeremy tilted his head to the side, studying her. Finally, he nodded decisively. "You're right. I'll just say it how I see it now." He cleared his throat. "I want to thank you for discrediting my abilities to my father. I want to thank you for humiliating me in front of my peers and superiors. And mostly, I want to thank you for ending my career in Hollywood."

two

"Excuse me?" The words bounced around Candice's mind, but she wasn't sure she'd heard Jeremy correctly. She glanced at the technicians to see if they'd overheard Jeremy's remarks, but they were still absorbed in their own conversation. Maybe her active guilt complex had switched all Jeremy's words around to sound so horrible. Yet the sick feeling that spread through her stomach confirmed her worst fears. Jeremy was another person from her past from whom she had to seek forgiveness. If only she could remember what she had done to him.

There had been so many people she'd crossed paths with whom she didn't remember. If the person didn't serve an immediate purpose, Candi had brushed him aside. Those people were expendable and inconsequential. Had Jeremy been one of those? Looking at Jeremy, Candice couldn't understand what she had been thinking. He was a nice-looking man, even with his scowl. Whether the scowl was caused by pain or distaste for her, Candice wasn't sure. "You say I ruined your career? I'm sorry. All I can say is how sorry I am." The words sounded inadequate and detached, but Candice couldn't muster any real feeling over something she couldn't remember.

Jeremy crossed his arms over his chest, then winced from his injuries and let his free arm drop slowly back. "You don't remember, do you?" he accused.

Candice regretfully shook her head. "I don't. I'm sorry."

Jeremy gave a humorless laugh. "Let me catch you up on old times. I imagined myself in love with you. Every guy in America felt the same way, I'm sure. Then I met you. Boy,

20

was my dream shattered. You ridiculed my work, then ordered my boss to get rid of me. I never imagined someone so beautiful could be so heartless. It was a day that forever changed my life." His voice wasn't hostile; neither did it contain any warmth.

Candice backed away, unsure of what Jeremy expected from her. She felt as if her heart might burst from the heavy burden of fresh guilt. She had ruined his life! "I know it isn't worth much now, Jeremy, but I really am sorry. I'm so sorry for what I did." She knew if she didn't leave she would make a fool of herself. Before Jeremy could respond, Candice turned and hurried out of the examination room. Tears of shame and regret clogged her throat as she hurried away as fast as she could.

Craig, her partner, was waiting for her not far from the first-aid station. He leaned casually against one of the ski racks as he talked with two young women. When he saw Candice coming toward him, he flashed her one of his heart-melting smiles. It had no effect on her, but it turned his two adoring fans green with jealousy. Candice was sure he did it only for the ego boost. He loved having women fight over him.

Candice quickly swiped at the tears on her cheeks. She didn't want him to see her crying. That would give him enough ammunition to use against her for the rest of the day. She zipped her coat and pulled on her gloves as she approached Craig.

"It's about time, Hollywood. I thought you were considering another career change with how long you took." Craig's haughty words came out as white puffs in the cold air.

Candice shook her head, unwilling to spar with Craig. "Which run do you want, Craig? I'll take the blues and blacks again."

Craig threw Candice a dangerous look. "Of course, you're

teasing. I don't mind taking the harder runs." He glanced at his two admirers, who didn't miss any of the interchange. "We both know I'm better suited to handle the rough terrain of those runs."

Candice turned from Craig, rolling her eyes and shaking her head. He knew that she was just as good a skier as he or she wouldn't have been selected for ski patrol. The last snatch of conversation she heard as she walked away was Craig's offer to ride the lift with the two women. She hoped that neither of the women would be so gullible as to go out with Craig. The five-minute lift ride would show them he only liked to talk about himself.

The rest of Candice's day went by without a hitch. Once she had to reprimand a pair of skiers for going outside the boundaries; otherwise it was a quiet day. After the last skier was off the mountain, Candice and the other ski patrol employees were free to go home. Candice collected her things from her locker, then headed toward her Subaru. On her way out she saw Craig with his arms wrapped around two young women. She felt sorry for them.

ভ

Candice's mind was just about clear of all guilt until she pulled up to her apartment. A strange, blue Dodge Sport pickup sat parked in her spot, but that wasn't too unusual. Her parking place had her apartment number on it, but no one noticed it because of the snow. As it was closest to the building, the spot was usually taken. Candice got out of her car and followed the snowy path to her apartment door. A shadowy figure lurked by her front door, and Candice paused in uncertainty.

The figure straightened and stepped into the light cast from the porch lamp. It was Jeremy. His arm was still in a sling, but he no longer wore ski clothes. Instead he had on slacks and a heavy coat. He gave Candice a hesitant wave.

"I don't think we got off to a good start today," he said as Candice came closer. "You didn't let me finish."

"You mean there's more?" Candice brushed past him to unlock her door. She was tired from a long cold day, and all she wanted was to snuggle in front of the fireplace with a mug of hot chocolate. She didn't want to remember who Jeremy was and what she'd done to him.

"Candi, we really need to talk. I want this resolved between us." Jeremy gripped Candice's arm and turned her toward him. Even through the thickness of her coat she could feel the warmth of his fingers. Candice looked up into his chocolate brown eyes. The sincerity she read made her gulp back any reservations she had.

"All right. You can come in. My roommate should be home anytime." She led him inside and into the kitchen.

Jeremy sat at the table as Candice moved around the kitchen, fixing two steaming mugs of hot cocoa. She felt nervous under his steady gaze, and she couldn't bring herself to look at him except for brief glimpses.

She liked how his brown hair always looked mussed as if he were a little boy who had just awoken from a nap. His brown eyes reminded her of deep pools of chocolate with shimmering lights in them. Tiny laugh lines framing his eyes creased more deeply when he smiled. She wished he were smiling now and not watching her with such intensity. If only he would say what was on his mind. Then she could apologize again, and it would be over.

After setting a mug in front of Jeremy, Candice reluctantly sat across the table from him. She took a sip from her own mug. The hot chocolate burned her lips and tongue.

"Ouch!" She jumped from her seat, ran to the sink, and quickly poured herself a cold glass of water. As she gulped the water, the burning sensation left her tongue. In the background she could hear Jeremy chuckle. She ignored his amusement and plopped back into the seat across from him.

"Better?" he asked.

Candice nodded. "Much." She picked up her mug again and took another, more hesitant, sip of the cocoa. She felt like a fool for her silly behavior. It surely didn't help improve Jeremy's impression of her.

Jeremy cleared his throat. "I need to start over. By your reaction this afternoon, I obviously bumbled what I wanted to tell you. So let's try again." He held out his hand to take Candice's. "My name is Jeremy Braunfeld. And you are?"

Candice noticed the twinkle in his eyes and decided to play along. She allowed him to grasp her fingers in his. "Candice Drakeforth."

"Candice. Not Candi anymore?" he asked.

Candice shook her head. "I'm Candi only to my family now. Rarely do I come across someone who recognizes me."

Jeremy squeezed her fingers as he nodded decisively. "Candice it is. I prefer it actually. It sounds more grown up, more graceful."

Unaccustomed to such compliments, Candice blushed under his watchful gaze. She hadn't blushed because of a man in years. "Tell me why I ruined your life, Jeremy. I'm sorry, but I honestly don't remember what happened."

Jeremy leaned back in his chair and crossed his arms. He looked comfortable in her kitchen, as though it was a regular occurrence for him to chat with her. "Let me start by saying that it wasn't entirely your fault. I had built you into something of an idol. I taped all of your commercials and watched them over and over. Remember those sweaters you modeled for? I collected every poster I could find and cut the ad out of all the magazines. I was so excited to actually work on a film you were in. I just knew when you met me that you would fall in love with me, just as I thought I was in love with you. I never imagined that you would blow up over a few little mistakes."

"What were the mistakes?" Candice asked. "Sorry, I don't remember."

Jeremy shrugged. "I helped edit the scenes after they were filmed. I left in some scenes you wanted cut. I guess you believed they were unflattering. You went screaming to the producer, my father, and ordered him to fire me on the spot. If he wouldn't fire me, you were going to walk out of the film. They couldn't lose you at that point because the film was three-quarters finished. I was expendable. So Pop handed me my walking papers. It was tough."

"I got you fired," Candice whispered.

"Yup. But that was then. It was actually a blessing. I just didn't realize it." Jeremy took a sip of his hot cocoa.

Candice pushed away her mug. "I don't see how it could have been a blessing. I hate how I acted! I was cruel and hateful. I used people. Jeremy, if I could make it up to you I would. I'm just helpless to make any restitution."

"Candice, getting fired was the best thing to happen to me. I've always been more interested in construction than in the movie industry. My uncle needed my help running his business, and I was about to start working with him when Pop recruited me. He thought he could mold me into his image, the great movie producer. I've always wanted to please the man, so I went along with his notions for awhile. I hated making those edits. I was a miserable match for the job. I don't have an eye for artistic expression. I can't tell what needs to stay and what needs to be cut. But I felt obligated to my father. He knew I couldn't do the job but didn't want to tell me, and I didn't want to quit and hurt him. You did us both a favor."

"You make me sound like a hero. I wasn't. I was awful. I just hope you can forgive me."

"Forgiving you is the easy part. Especially now. You seem different. Maybe it's because we've both grown up."

Candice shook her head. "No, I can tell you why I'm different. It's because I've recommitted my life to the Lord. I'm no longer trying to advance in my acting career at another person's expense. In fact, I rarely think of that career. What a change, huh? I bet you never imagined Candi Drakeforth as ski patrol."

Jeremy shook his head with a laugh. "You're right! For awhile I couldn't even think of you period. You're like a breath of fresh air now." He rose and carried his mug to the sink. "Before it starts snowing again, I need to get over to my hotel. Thankfully it's really close. My head is starting to pound again."

"You took quite a fall. Take it easy for a few days, and you'll be back on skis in no time."

Jeremy shook his head with a laugh. "Not likely. Not unless I take ski lessons."

Candice rose and walked Jeremy to the door. She held out her hand in a friendly gesture. Jeremy took her hand between his, holding it longer than necessary. He reluctantly released it and took a step back.

"I'll see you, Candice. Thanks for inviting me in."

Candice nodded and watched him walk down the path. She liked Jeremy Braunfeld. If they had met under different circumstances, she may have tried to get to know him. But that could never be. She watched his retreating form until the path took him out of her vision.

"Thanks for forgiving me, Jeremy," Candice said, though she couldn't see him any longer. She leaned her head against the door and closed her eyes. "Only a thousand more people left to go."

❧

Jeremy skipped down the walk—well, skip wasn't exactly the

right word. Lobbed along was a better description. His knee was pretty sore, but he didn't care about the pain. He felt euphoric! Ecstatic! Very pleased at the least. He briefly closed his eyes, and a sweet image of a beautiful woman emerged in his mind's eye.

Candi Drakeforth. No, wait. She was Candice now. She was everything he remembered by appearance with her silky blond hair, gorgeous green eyes that reminded him of a Bengal tiger about to pounce, and those sweet rosy lips. How many nights had he dreamed of having a conversation with her? A few years ago he had worshipped the ground she walked on, though worship wasn't quite the right term. He'd adored her. She could do no wrong. Then the day came when her image shattered.

It had been a good thing, as he'd just told Candice. Jeremy remembered the day as though it were yesterday. She had been irate over the film edits. And to give her credit, he could have done a better job if he had enjoyed the work more and if he had any natural ability. But he was a klutz when it came to editing. His father knew it, Jeremy knew it, and only Candi was willing to interfere and state it as she saw it. And yes, she did state her opinion. Loudly. Jeremy could remember the beautiful blond with green eyes flashing as she stomped into his father's office. He could still hear her screaming harsh words.

Everyone had turned sympathetic eyes toward Jeremy. He hated the sympathy. They all knew what it was like to work with her. She was such a perfectionist, and she rarely gave any credit to a job well done. No one could please her, especially not Jeremy. After she stormed out of the building, everyone could hear the tires squeal on her sports car as she tore out of the parking lot. Jeremy thought her temper tantrum was a little extreme, but he wasn't about to say anything against the princess. Without her, there would be no movie.

Once the coast was clear, Jeremy walked into his father's office. With one look at his father's grim expression, Jeremy knew he was defeated.

"I'm sorry, Son," his father had said. "She's right. We need a better man in here to do the job. She said it's either you or her. And I have to say good-bye to you. No hard feelings?"

Jeremy had shrugged. Sure, his ego was deflated and trampled under her pretty little feet. It stung to be fired by his own father. But Jeremy had his walking papers, and he was finally free to do what he wanted. It was a good day.

"No hard feelings, Pop," Jeremy had answered.

After that memorable day, Jeremy had difficulty thinking of Candi Drakeforth in a positive light. As he'd packed to leave California, he'd thrown away all his posters, snapshots, magazine articles—everything with Candi's face on it. He was finished dreaming of her.

After all those years, it had been a shock to see Candice at the party. Since she had faded from the Hollywood scene, no one had ever heard from her again. A while ago he'd asked his father what had happened to her, but no one knew where she was. Now Jeremy knew; she was in Colorado skiing. It wasn't a career he would have imagined for her in a million years. He also wouldn't have imagined her to be so sweet. Their last encounter had left a sour taste for him, but now she was different. He could clearly see the change, and he was intrigued by it. He knew he had to see her again. Tomorrow would not be too soon. He went to sleep with her sweet image in his mind.

three

Candice groaned and rolled over in bed. It had been another sleepless night. Over and over she thought of all the people in her past whom she had hurt. Now she could easily remember the events that Jeremy had described. She recalled her smug satisfaction that she'd had a hand in it. All the looks of shock, disapproval, hatred that had been directed at her came to the forefront of her thoughts. As quickly as she remembered Jeremy's story, she switched to her own embarrassing day in the movie industry. She truly understood how humiliated he must have felt. When she'd stood before her own audience of critics, she'd wanted to sink through the floor. And worse, the one person she'd loved and trusted above all, her fiancé, had been the person leading the jeers.

"Candice, wake up! I can't believe you're still in bed!"

Candice rolled over to find Lindsey standing in the doorway, tapping her foot. In response to her roommate's pointed stare, Candice pulled the blankets over her head.

"Candice! Don't you know what day it is?"

"Sunday," Candice mumbled from beneath the covers. "My day off."

"Wrong!" Lindsey ripped the blankets from the bed, leaving Candice curled up and clutching her pillow. "You have twenty minutes before the winter carnival begins. Hurry up and get ready!"

"All right." Candice reluctantly got up from the bed. With her restless night, she had forgotten all about the winter carnival the town held every year for children. If she didn't feel so weary, she'd be excited about the carnival. Even her small church held services in the park during the carnival. She and Lindsey volunteered, but Candice couldn't remember what she'd been assigned to do. Maybe she would have to make toasted sandwiches. Anything warm would be nice.

"Come on, Candice, it's time to go," Lindsey called from the living room. Candice threw on some clothes, tied back her hair, then pulled on her boots.

"I'm ready!" She rushed with Lindsey out the door and over to the park.

The winter carnival was something all the locals looked forward to. It featured snowmobile rides, a small petting zoo, an ice-skating pond, a sledding hill, and cross-country ski races. Concession stands selling hot cocoa, toasted sandwiches, and cinnamon rolls were staffed by volunteers. Other volunteers gave free ski lessons to children. Mostly they just pulled the little kids around on skis, but the children really enjoyed it.

"What are we doing this year, Lindsey?" Candice asked as they trudged through the fresh snow toward the carnival. In the distance they could hear braying ponies and excited shouting. Some teenagers were raising bright flags and banners.

"I'm serving cinnamon rolls. I believe you are monitoring the sledding run." Lindsey flipped her short brown hair. "I'm hoping to land one of those rich townsmen. Then I won't have to spend my days helping with ski school."

"I bet you'll have so much fun today, you'll forget about husband hunting, Lindsey." They were approaching the sledding run, and Candice slowed her steps. "Don't forget me when you're serving that cocoa. By the end of the day, my fingers and toes will be frozen."

"I'll bring you a sandwich and hot chocolate at noon. How does that sound?"

"Perfect!" Candice answered over her shoulder. She and

Lindsey parted ways, and Candice hurried to her post. Children with sleds were already lined up, awaiting her arrival. The kids, all bundled in winter gear, huddled at the bottom of the long slope. Candice could see they'd come prepared. Some had large, bouncy inner tubes. She saw two little boys with round discs. There was an old-fashioned wood sled and a couple toboggans. It promised to be a fun day.

Candice approached the excited group of children. "Let's go over the guidelines before we get started. Okay, kids?" Enthusiastic shouts and titters came from the group. "Great! Now we all want to have fun, so let's make sure we stay safe. First, nobody is to walk up the middle of the run. Stay to the sides of the slope. If you fall off your sled, move to the side so you don't get hit. No roughhousing, of course. And please don't build any snow mounds. Little kids can get hurt if they hit a mound and go flying. The run is narrow, so only one sled should be launched at a time. Too many sleds and people get hit. More than one person can ride a sled if you choose. If you get hurt and have any problems, I'll be here at the bottom watching. So go have fun!"

With a collective whoop, the children hauled their sleds up the steep slope. The run was good, wide enough that the sleds rarely went toward the trees and steep enough for good speed. The snow was packed but not icy. As a precaution, hay bales encircled the closest trees. If a sled went off course, nobody would get seriously hurt.

Soon kids were flying down the hill. Laughter pierced the air, drawing more children. A few adults joined in the fun. Parents lined the "finish line" to watch their children speed down the slope. Candice envied the children's endless resources of energy as they trudged up the hill time and again. She knew how much hard work it took to pull the sleds, but the thrilling ride down was worth the effort.

Candice was so engrossed with watching the sledding that she didn't hear someone approach her.

"Candice."

Startled, Candice turned to find Jeremy standing near her with a Styrofoam cup of steaming cocoa. Candice's gaze was magnetically drawn to his, and she couldn't pull away. He looked better than the last time she'd seen him after his skiing injury. The white bandage no longer adorned his forehead. A bruise surrounded the long cut the bandage had protected, and it looked sore. His arm was still in a sling, but he didn't appear to be in much pain. At least he was smiling.

"Mr. Braunfeld, have you brought me cocoa?" Candice asked. She couldn't help the teasing lilt in her voice. It was a festive day, and she had caught the mood.

"Why, yes, Miss Drakeforth, I have. I ran into your friend, Lindsey. She said you might need a little warmth."

Candice shivered, though she was accustomed to the cold. "Actually, yes. I could use a little warmth." As Candice accepted the cup of cocoa, she blushed under Jeremy's intense gaze.

"Perhaps we could go someplace warm when you're done here," he suggested.

Candice took a sip of the cocoa. She could feel the warm liquid go down, warming her insides. "Maybe. How long will you be here, Jeremy?" She didn't like to get involved with vacationers. They were never on the mountain long enough to start a meaningful relationship. Anything less than meaningful wasn't worth her time.

Jeremy shrugged. "Actually, I'll be here for quite awhile. I'm building some new condos over there." He pointed toward a ridge west of town. "I'm glad I won't be the one wielding a hammer, since I crashed and burned. This sore shoulder ruined my plans of becoming an expert skier."

"More condos are just what this town needs. There aren't

enough places for all the resort employees to live once they secure positions. Hopefully they will be affordable."

"I'm doing my best to keep the costs reasonable. Nothing comes cheap these days. So how about meeting somewhere later?" he pressed.

Despite her normal reservations, Candice felt drawn to Jeremy and found herself agreeing to his idea. "I know a nice little café most of the tourists never find. It's quiet. We could go there," she suggested.

Jeremy beamed at Candice. "Perfect! Maybe we can just talk for awhile. I'd like to get to know you better."

"Thanks, Jeremy. Me too."

Candice was so distracted by Jeremy that she wasn't paying as much attention to the rowdy sledders as she should. Neither of them noticed the sled careening down the hill straight toward them at full speed.

Out of the corner of her eye, Candice noticed movement. The heavy wood sled with red metal runners was speeding down the hill straight toward them.

"Watch out, Jeremy!" She pushed Jeremy hard, and he fell to the side, out of the path of the runaway sled. Unfortunately, Candice remained in its path. The sled plowed into Candice's legs, knocking her on her back. She hit her head on something, she knew, because she felt a sharp pain in the back of her head. Then all went black.

❧

Something gentle and feather soft tickled Candice's cheek. It wasn't an unpleasant sensation, just unfamiliar.

"Candice, can you hear me? Open your eyes," someone pleaded.

Candice turned her face toward the voice and tried to comply. Her eyelids felt heavy, as though bags of sand weighed them down.

"Come on, Candice, try to look at me. I need to know you're okay."

Candice could hear the growing desperation and did as bid. Bright light blinded her vision as she squinted at the person leaning over her. It took a moment for her vision to clear but she was finally able to focus on Jeremy's face above hers. "Hi, Jeremy," she whispered, and she could hear his sigh of relief.

"She's okay," someone called out. Candice could see a crowd had gathered around her. After the announcement of the good news, they slowly dispersed.

Candice pushed away Jeremy's supporting arm and tried to sit. Her head spun with the effort. Jeremy kept his arm against her back to steady her. "My head hurts," she complained.

With gentle fingers, Jeremy probed the tender flesh at the back of Candice's head. When he hit the sore spot, Candice flinched.

"Sorry, I'm sure it hurts. You have a pretty big goose egg. I think I should take you to the doctor."

Candice shook her head, wincing as pain shot through her head. "No, I'm fine. No doctor."

"But you were knocked unconscious, Candice! You of all people know you need to see a doctor. You take every injured skier straight to the doctor. Don't you think you should go and have this looked at?"

"Jeremy, your concern is sweet, but honestly I'm fine."

"Candice, please. Just let someone take a look and make sure you're okay."

"I'm not seeing a doctor. He'll tell me I have a big bump. I already know that. If I notice any side effects from this I'll see the doctor at the resort." Jeremy appeared skeptical. "I promise, Jeremy!"

"If you're sure. I can't make you go."

Candice smiled at his reluctant agreement. "Jeremy, help me find what I hit my head on. It felt like a rock."

They searched the immediate area, and Candice spotted a large rock peeking out of the snow. "I can't believe there's a rock on this sledding hill. I'm glad all I got was a bump. Some kid could have really gotten hurt."

She watched as Jeremy dug into the snow and pulled out the rock. It was about the size of a football. Jeremy carried the rock off the sled run and into the trees. When he came back, he held out a hand to help Candice to her feet. Candice gladly accepted his help. She brushed the snow off her clothes and clapped her mittens together, sending up a small cloud of powdery snow.

Jeremy brushed off his own clothes. "Why don't we go find that quiet café? After that little accident, I'll bet you're done for the day."

Candice nodded, rubbing the tender spot on her head. "If you'll go tell Lindsey what happened, I'm sure she can find me a replacement. I'm ready to be out of the cold."

A short while later, Jeremy led them to his pickup, and they drove the short distance to Candice's favorite café. Before she could get out of the vehicle, Jeremy had the passenger door open to help her out. He took her hand to assist her. And he didn't break the contact with her until they reached the front door of the café. She didn't comment on his forward action, nor did she resist it. She didn't know why she was even with him except that he intrigued her. She wanted to know why he forgave her so easily for hurting him in the past. It made no sense to her that he bore her no ill will.

Though the café was nearly empty, probably because of the winter carnival, Jeremy selected a table in a secluded corner. He pulled out a chair for Candice, then sat across from her. A waitress quickly approached their table.

"Can I start you with some warm cider?" she asked.

Both Jeremy and Candice shook their heads. Candice winced at the sudden pain. "I think the lady could use an ice bag and a packet of aspirin, if you have it available," Jeremy suggested.

The waitress swung her gaze toward Candice. "Sure thing, Hon. You feelin' all right?"

Candice nodded, more gently this time. "I'm going to be just fine. And I'd like a hot turkey sandwich and a cup of coffee with that aspirin."

"You got it." The waitress turned to Jeremy. "And you, young man? Do you want an aspirin too? It looks like you could use one."

It was true that Jeremy looked uncomfortable because of his skiing injuries. He tried to laugh off their concern. "No aspirin. But I'll take the turkey sandwich and coffee too."

"No problem. I'll be right back with that aspirin." The waitress tucked her pencil in her apron and hurried back to the kitchen. Candice let her gaze roam over Jeremy's face. Though he tried to hide it, Candice could see he was in pain.

"Jeremy, did you fall on your arm when I pushed you?"

Jeremy shrugged, careful of his shoulder. "You saved my life."

"Hardly!" Candice laughed. "I just knocked you out of the way of a couple of kids. It wasn't life threatening."

"Maybe not life threatening, but it was harmful enough to give you a whopper of a headache," Jeremy argued. "I think we're quite a pair. You and I should retire from winter sports for awhile."

"I'm just glad a child didn't get hurt. It was better my tough head found that rock," Candice mused.

"Why do you say that? Of course I don't want any kids to get hurt, but you didn't deserve to get hurt either."

"Maybe I did deserve it," Candice answered quietly. She

stared at the paisley pattern of the tablecloth, unable to meet Jeremy's gaze. When he remained silent, she cautiously glanced at him.

"You can't mean that," he answered, his voice equally soft yet firm with conviction.

Candice shrugged, wanting to change the subject, but Jeremy wouldn't comply. "Nobody deserves to get hurt. Why do you think that?"

"Let me ask you something, Jeremy. Do you think God punishes us for the wrongs we commit?"

"God disciplines those He loves," Jeremy began slowly. "And there are always consequences for our actions whether we are Christians or not. But I don't believe God ever punishes us unjustly out of anger. That goes against His characteristics. That's where grace comes in and that's also why Jesus died for our sins—"

He broke off as the waitress returned with two mugs of coffee, a cup of water, and a packet of aspirin. "Your sandwiches will be up in just a moment," she said as she turned back toward the kitchen.

Candice swallowed the aspirin with a quick gulp of water. "God's grace is something I don't think I'll ever understand." She gave a small shrug, wanting to lighten the mood. "Tell me how you got into building condos for a living now that you don't edit film."

Candice could tell Jeremy wasn't ready to change the topic, but he didn't pursue it further. "My Uncle Jon and I have always had a close relationship, something my father didn't understand. My father wanted me to follow in his footsteps of movie producing. I wanted to work with my uncle. When my father finally accepted that I wasn't cut out for movie making, he let me go follow my own desires."

He paused as the waitress placed two plates piled with hot

turkey sandwiches on the table before them. After a brief prayer over the food, Jeremy continued. "My uncle was more than ready to take me onboard. He's been grooming me to take over the business these last few years. This condominium project is actually my first solo venture."

"What is involved with being a builder? You said you wouldn't be the one with a hammer."

"Right. I'm kind of a project foreman. I get the buyer's preferences, hire the work crews, and oversee the building. Sometimes I have to be in five places at once, and it can be rather challenging, but I really enjoy the work."

"I'm glad you found your niche, Jeremy. I'm still looking for mine." Candice grabbed her paper napkin and started folding it into triangles. "I like to ski, and I enjoy working for the resort. Actually, I don't know if it has anything to do with my job." She shrugged self-consciously. "Never mind. I know I'm not making any sense."

Jeremy leaned forward, staring intently into Candice's eyes, and she could tell that he didn't want to drop the conversation. Just as he started to speak, she jumped to her feet.

"Would you like to return to the winter carnival? We could browse around nice and slow," she suggested. "There are different booths set up all over the park. And they even had a few new ones this year that I'd like to see."

Once Jeremy settled the bill, they exited the café and got in his truck to drive back to the carnival.

As Jeremy eased his pickup onto the dirt-packed road he stole a glance at Candice. "Can I ask you something?"

Candice's thoughts flew to her bumbling words at the café and how she hadn't found her niche. Hopefully he wasn't going to pick up that conversation. Those thoughts should never have surfaced, especially with someone she hardly knew. There were things from her past that she wasn't ready to deal with. She hadn't even shared them with her sister. "Okay, ask," she cautiously answered.

"What made you give up acting? Ski patrol is a long way from shooting commercials and movies. You were very good at what you did."

Memories flashed through Candice's mind as though they'd occurred yesterday and not three years ago. The fan mail used to pile up at her agent's office. She loved having celebrity magazines write articles about her and her thriving career. Fast cars, famous men, money—it had been a whirlwind lifestyle. Then it came to a shattering halt. Part of her missed the acting. She loved the challenge of learning her lines and stepping into a role that was so far removed from her real life. Yet in her mind she couldn't separate the lifestyle from the career.

"It's very simple. God finally got ahold of me. I was going in the wrong direction at the speed of an express train. When the train crashed, there was no way to repair the damage. All I could do was leave the business," she said with a touch of regret. "I suppose I had it coming after the way I treated so many people. I just didn't see it coming until it happened."

"Something happened?"

Candice could picture Edwardo Estanza and all the others laughing at her during the failed audition. Some discreetly hid their smiles behind their hands, others outright shamed her. How could she have forgotten her lines? Edwardo should have put his arm around her and comforted her. Instead he pointed his finger and laughed. The old humiliation roiled, and the anxiety and hurt tried to push their way to the surface. Candice grabbed the armrest of the truck in a steely grip as she forced her thoughts from the past. She didn't want to deal with it. It still hurt too much. "Yes, Jeremy, something happened. But it was a long time ago. It doesn't matter anymore."

Jeremy eyed her quizzically. "Are you sure it doesn't matter?"

Candice nodded firmly, ending the conversation. Yet she had a feeling the discussion was far from over.

Silently, as though he were pondering her words, Jeremy parked the pickup in the lot. A blast of cold air greeted them as they left the warm interior of the truck. Jeremy reached for Candice's hand, and they walked together to watch the winter carnival participants. It didn't take long to spot Lindsey handing out balloons to all the little kids. They followed the bunch of red, purple, blue, and yellow balloons until they came to its source.

Lindsey waved to Candice and Jeremy as she saw them approach. "Hey, you two! I didn't think you would be back. You should be in the hot tub after getting plowed by that sled."

Candice shrugged. "Did we miss anything good?"

"It's all been good!" Lindsey launched into a broad description of the day's events. "And the best part was the snowshoe race. The mayor even entered. He almost came in last, but his assistant was in the race too, and he fell down at the last minute. I think he threw the race to keep his job," Lindsey finished with a giggle. "And the next event is couples skating. Why don't you enter, Candice?" she suggested with a wink.

Candice glowered at her friend. "I don't think I'm up for that much fun. But I'll watch the others." Candice grabbed Jeremy's hand and led him away before Lindsey could share any embarrassing stories about Candice's ice skating ability. Or rather inability.

As they walked toward the skating rink, Jeremy asked, "If you were feeling better, would you enter the skating contest?"

"No way! Skating is definitely not my sport."

"Ahh, come on, Candice. I'll bet you're good at all these winter sports. You're just being modest."

"Believe what you want, but there's no way you'll get me on that ice," Candice warned. She watched the contestants glide around the frozen pond. None of them were professionals, but they stayed on their feet much better than Candice could have. Couples continued to zoom around the small pond. Some skated backwards, others did different turns and spins. Candice became so absorbed with the skaters that she jumped when Jeremy bent to whisper in her ear. "I'll teach you to ice skate if you'll teach me to ski."

Candice turned to find Jeremy's face just inches from her own. All rational thought flew from her mind as she stared into the bottomless depths of his dark brown eyes. "You want to teach me to ice skate?"

Jeremy nodded slowly, never taking his gaze from hers. "Do we have a deal?"

"Okay," Candice whispered. She moved fractionally closer to him, not seeking a kiss, but to feel nearer to him. Jeremy understood her desire and put his arm around her shoulders, cradling her close against his side. Together, they finished watching the skating competition. Yet neither could remember anything about the winners.

four

The phone was ringing as Candice walked into her apartment. Jeremy had just dropped her off and was on his way back to his hotel. She wondered if his shoulder injury might interfere with his work. He certainly wouldn't be able to ski for the next few days. She was glad he wasn't on a ski vacation. Candice wanted the chance to know him and hoped he would drop by occasionally. She was through being aggressive and making the first move with men. She wanted to spend more time with Jeremy, but if he didn't come around, she wouldn't pursue him. He had shown interest in teaching her to ice skate. Hopefully he meant what he suggested and wasn't just making conversation.

Racing to the phone, Candice was breathless when she answered. "Hello?"

"Hey, Candi!"

Candice relaxed when she heard the familiar sound of her sister's voice. "Claire! Is everything all right?"

"Perfectly fine. That is, I think everything is fine," Claire answered. "I just got an interesting call that I thought you should know about. I think Edwardo is trying to find you."

"What?" Candice felt her heart skip a beat at the mention of her ex-fiancé's name.

"That guy you were engaged to, Edwardo. I think he called. It sounded like him, but he wouldn't give me his name. He asked a bunch of questions about you."

"Questions?" Candice parroted. "What did he want to know?"

Some static interfered with the line, but Claire's voice came through faintly. "He wanted to know if you're married, if you're

42

still acting, where you're living. Those types of questions. I didn't tell him anything. The entire conversation made me nervous. He got angry with me and said he would find out what he wanted to know without my help, then he hung up. What do you think it means?"

A ball of anxiety rolled in the pit of Candice's stomach. "I don't know what it means, but please pray, Claire."

"I will, Love. Please keep Rick and me informed."

Candice set the phone down with shaking fingers. Just as the line clicked, she remembered that she hadn't told Claire anything about Jeremy. The news about Edwardo had her so upset that everything else had been pushed to the back of her mind. Maybe it hadn't been Edwardo who had questioned Claire, Candice reasoned. The caller hadn't revealed his name. Yet there was no one else she could think of who would want to know anything about her. Why would Edwardo want to contact her after so many years? He was supposed to be married. That news had crushed her because he was the first man she hadn't used. She'd actually loved him.

Sagging into a chair, Candice breathed a prayer. "Please, Lord, don't let Edwardo come back into my life. I've just gotten things in order. I don't think I can handle seeing him again. And also, Lord, thank You for Jeremy. I feel very blessed that he has forgiven me. God, please help me get past my sins of yesterday. I never seem to be rid of them, and I'm weary from carrying the load. I'm tired of the overwhelming guilt and hurt and anger I always feel."

≈

After a long night's sleep Candice felt refreshed and better than she had the evening before. Her headache from the sledding accident was gone, and all that remained was a large tender bump on the back of her head. Thoughts of Edwardo tried to crowd into her mind, but Candice quickly forced them away. She didn't want to think about Edwardo and why he might search for her. She didn't want anything to ruin her day. It was a beautiful morning, though dark since it was only four-thirty.

Candice threw on a heavy sweatshirt, stuffed everything she needed for the workday into her backpack, then headed for the door. Just as she was about to leave, Lindsey stumbled into the room, rubbing her eyes.

"Why are you up?" she asked through a yawn. "Is it still Sunday?"

"No, Silly. It's Monday. I'm scheduled to work, so I thought I would go for a run before I check in. I get to hang out with the snowmobiles today, so if I want any exercise, I'd better get it now," Candice answered cheerfully.

Lindsey turned to go back to her room, mumbling something about her crazy roommate.

Easing out of the apartment so as not to wake any of the other sleeping tenants, Candice struck out at a slow pace. The cold air invigorated her as she widened her steps to stretch her muscles. She remembered how her sister, Claire, and their father used to go running together. Candice had always scoffed at them because she hadn't wanted to exert herself. Now she enjoyed the exercise. She wished her parents lived a little closer than Montana. It would be nice to have a jogging partner.

Candice's shoes made soft crunching sounds in the snow as she picked up speed. The road she selected was a two-mile stretch to the ski resort. She planned to reach the resort, change in the ladies' room, then have a quick breakfast before she had to check in for work. The banana and granola bar bouncing around in her backpack would be just enough to get her by until lunch.

Nearing the halfway point on the road to the resort, Candice heard a car coming behind her. She moved to the side of the road near the tree line because she knew a driver wouldn't expect to see someone running at such an early hour. The road became steeper, and Candice had to concentrate on her pace and breathing. She matched her inhaling and exhaling with each pounding stride. The snow was packed hard so she had to be careful not to slip. The car pulled behind her, lighting her path with its headlights. Candice expected the car to pass, but it hung behind her. Slowly it crept closer to Candice, staying only three or four feet behind her.

Sweat began to trickle down Candice's back as her heart rate increased from fear. The car continued to follow her. Candice glanced over her shoulder, but the headlights blinded her, and she couldn't make out any details of the car or the driver.

Unsure of the driver's intentions, Candice decided to get off the road. Probably there was nothing to be concerned about, but she wasn't taking any chances. She quickly scaled the bank of snow made by the snowplows, then ran down a steep embankment into the trees. Without going many feet she sunk to her knees in the soft powdery snow. She took a moment to catch her breath and figure what to do about her new predicament. She decided it would be foolhardy to try to trek through the woods where the snow was powdery and deep. She would grow cold and exhausted and might lose her way. She needed to get back on the road. Struggling, she took one giant step, quickly sinking into the powder, then another step.

"At this rate, I might make it to work by next Thursday," Candice muttered.

Slowly she made it back to the edge of the embankment where she had slid down from the road. The car was no longer in sight, making her frantic efforts seem foolish.

"Okay, Candice Drakeforth, where did all that survival training go? You know better than to run blindly into a forest."

The thought of the car following her so closely reminded

her that her actions had not been foolish. It had turned out to be nothing, but she wondered why the driver had followed her so closely. Did he think he recognized her? Was he just startled to see a jogger so early and wanted to make sure she was okay? Perhaps he was lost. There were a million and one reasons that could justify the incident.

After taking one slow step at a time, Candice finally made it back up the embankment and onto the road. Covered with snow, she felt cold and hungry. Her run didn't seem nearly as appealing as it had earlier, but there was no turning back. Slowly she set out, making each foot move in front of the other in regular rhythm. The sun was beginning to come up, and the sky was growing lighter. Candice was glad the morning was on its way, but it also meant she needed to hurry if she was to have her breakfast before work.

Finally, reaching the resort, Candice hurried to the employees' locker rooms. She quickly changed into her ski clothes in the ladies' room, then she ate her banana and granola bar.

After breakfast Candice felt better prepared to face her day. Though it had started off in an odd and unsettling way, she knew a day was what she made it to be. And she determined to make it a good one.

"You look terrible, Movie Queen," Craig greeted Candice as she walked into the ski patrol office.

"This will be a good day no matter what," Candice muttered under her breath as she faced Craig. Even though he was a pain, she would not let him get under her skin. "Good morning to you too. Your compliments inspire me, Craig. No wonder the women flock to you."

Craig glowered at Candice but didn't comment. Instead he turned his attention to their supervisor, who walked through the doorway. Earl Masterson, or "Chief," tapped his clipboard against his hand as he looked around the room at his employees.

At the age of sixty-five, he was old enough to be a father to most of the skiers there, a fact he used to his advantage. No one ever underestimated or took advantage of Chief. To every new employee, Chief seemed like a brutal warhorse, but it didn't take long to find out that he was a softy on the inside. He liked to give fatherly advice, and he was always fair and understanding. Candice couldn't ask for a better boss.

"Morning, folks. You'll see the new schedule on the board. Need to make changes? Work it out yourself." Chief pulled his ball cap from his head, ran a hand over his thinning gray hair, then replaced the cap. He noticed Candice and pointed at her. "Come here, Candice. I need to talk to you about something."

Candice followed Chief into his office and shut the door behind her.

"What is it, Chief?"

Chief crossed his arms over his chest and leaned against his desk. He nodded toward a vacant chair, and Candice slid onto it. "Someone called here yesterday, looking for you. They called the main line of the resort, and the operator directed his call to my office. It was a detective. Is there something going on that I should know about?"

Candice nervously shook her head. First Claire had said Edwardo had called; now a detective was tracking her down at work. What was going on? "I don't know what it's about, Chief. My sister said she got a strange call too. You didn't tell him anything, did you?"

"Nope. He wasn't on official police business with a warrant, so I didn't feel inclined to share any confidential information. He doesn't know you work here, but I'm sure he figured that out before he called. I'm not sure what he was after." Chief patted Candice's shoulder reassuringly. "I just wanted you to know."

Candice smiled weakly at her boss. "Thanks, Chief. I'm not

sure what this is about, but I know I'll find out soon enough. Either way, I trust God to protect me."

Chief nodded as he ushered her out of the office. "That's right. And don't you forget it."

As Candice grabbed her gear to meet up with the team she was assigned to, Craig stopped her in the doorway. "Hey, Movie Queen. Some guy was looking for you this morning before you got here. What did you do, oversleep?"

Candice thought of her early morning run, the mysterious car, and her trek in the snow. Had she overslept? Hardly! "What did he look like?"

Craig shrugged. "I don't know. You can't expect me to remember things like that."

"Did he have black hair and dark eyes? Was he Hispanic?" Candice pressed.

"Like I said, I don't know. Now let me tell you about the blond I met last night—"

Candice held up her hand to silence Craig. "Later. It's time for me to find my team."

Thoughts of strange cars, detectives, and unknown callers nagged at Candice all day. She was glad there weren't too many emergencies requiring her assistance. The two guys on her team volunteered for most of the calls, leaving Candice alone at the base of the mountain. She didn't mind since she felt weary from her concern. She hoped Edwardo wasn't behind all the sudden interest in her. She didn't know what she would do if he reappeared in her life. The last time she'd seen him had been the worst day of her life, and she had worked every day since to forget him.

❧

Jeremy waited as the clerk at the county office looked over the paperwork he had submitted. On the wall behind her desk, a small round clocked ticked loudly. He stared at it, watching each minute tick by with agonizing slowness. He had been at the county building for almost an hour, and most of that time had been spent waiting in line. Review of a building permit should not take that long.

However, there are some things worth waiting for, Jeremy thought with a smile. Candice Drakeforth was definitely worth waiting for. He couldn't wait to see her again. In his opinion she was even more beautiful than she had been when she was making movies and commercials. Her hair was longer and made him want to run his fingers through it just to see how soft it was. She wore very little makeup, allowing her natural beauty to shine through. And the attitude was gone. She no longer strutted around like a peacock flaunting its colorful feathers. It seemed to him that she had finally come to terms with who she was and that, of course, was all because of the Lord. He had changed her; that was true.

Jeremy was snapped out of his reverie when the clerk handed him copies of his paperwork.

"I'm sorry, Sir, there is a problem with your permit."

Jeremy frowned. "What do you mean, 'a problem'? I had this filed weeks ago. Am I just supposed to stop building because there is suddenly a problem?"

The clerk nodded. "I'm sorry, Sir, but it appears that some of your information was not filed correctly into our records. I assure you that it was not your oversight. Unfortunately, until these things are taken care of, I cannot reissue the permit."

Trying to control his agitation, Jeremy asked, "How long of a hold up are you suggesting? A few weeks?" The thought of that many days with his project on hold curled his stomach. He had contracted laborers waiting to work and building supplies ready to be used. A few weeks could really complicate things.

"Oh no, Sir!" the clerk said, shaking her head. "This will take only two days at the most. Probably less. Check back tomorrow morning and hopefully your paperwork will be updated."

Jeremy rose from his seat, clutching the paperwork. "Great! It's nice to have a day off. I'll be back tomorrow then." Taking the day off was just what the doctor had ordered as far as he was concerned. Ideas whirled in his mind. First he would go to Candice's apartment and see if she might spend the day with him. Maybe he could even persuade her to let him teach her to ice skate.

To his disappointment, Jeremy didn't find Candice at her apartment. Her sleepy, tousled roommate said that Candice was at work. He should have known she would have to work, but in his exuberance he hadn't even thought of it.

"But if you hurry, you can still catch her at the ski patrol office. I think she said she's on snowmobiles today so she'll be hanging around the base longer," Lindsey called as Jeremy hurried down the snowy path to his pickup. He waved over his shoulder at Lindsey. *Good!* he thought. *Maybe I can catch up with her and make plans for tonight.*

❧

Jeremy found Candice sitting on one of the Arctic Cat snow-mobiles outside the ski patrol office. She stared intently up at the snow-covered mountain and didn't seem to be aware of anything or anybody around her. Jeremy followed her gaze to the slope where skiers looked like tiny dots zigging and zagging down the mountain. Nothing seemed to be out of the ordinary to him, but maybe Candice saw something that he didn't. He clamped his hand down on Candice's shoulder to get her attention.

"What?!" Candice nearly fell off the snowmobile, she was so startled. Jeremy gripped her arm and helped her regain her balance.

"I didn't mean to scare you," Jeremy apologized. "What were you looking at?" he asked, turned back to the slope.

Candice laughed self-consciously as she brushed her hair out of her eyes. "I wasn't really looking at anything. Just daydreaming I guess." Her voice sounded a little strained, and the serious look in her eyes didn't match her attempt at lightheartedness.

Jeremy knelt beside her, unmindful of the powdery snow. "Why are you so jumpy? There's something wrong, isn't there?" A wisp of fear curled around Jeremy's heart. He didn't want to be rejected by this woman again.

Candice laughed and shrugged evasively. "I'm not jumpy. You just caught me off guard."

Jeremy's eyes narrowed. "I have a feeling there's more to it than you're telling me. You can trust me, Candice."

Candice stiffened, and her expression became impersonal as she stared back at him. "Jeremy, you don't know me as well as you think. Do you believe a few hours together gives you insight into my personality? You don't know me at all!" she said stiffly.

Jeremy winced at the sharp remark. "Some things take time, true." His voice faltered. "But other things you just know, Candice. Like how much I care for you. Some things you just know." He felt shaky and off balance like he had when she'd gotten him fired. He rose and took a few steps away from her. "But I can see you want your space, so I'll back off. If you need me, I'll be at the building site over the ridge." He tried to keep his voice even, but inside it felt as if she had taken his heart and crushed it under her boot. Perhaps she hadn't changed at all. At least she didn't yell and draw everyone's attention this time. He walked a few steps away, trying to deal with letting her go if that was what she wanted.

"Wait, Jeremy! Please wait!" Candice called after him. Slowly he walked back to her. She stared up at him with beseeching eyes. "Please don't be angry with me. I do have something on my mind, and it has me troubled, but I don't think now is the time to talk about it. Can I meet with you later?"

Unable to help himself, Jeremy reached over with gentle fingers and removed stray wisps of hair from Candice's forehead. She didn't flinch or back away, and Jeremy was glad his touch was welcome. "Maybe we could have a quiet dinner together and talk then," he suggested.

Candice nodded eagerly. "Yes, I think that's a good idea. Would you like to come over to my apartment? My roommate always has people stopping by, so it won't be quiet. But we could stay in the kitchen. I'm not such a bad cook."

Jeremy leaned forward and pressed a kiss on Candice's cheek. "It's a date."

≥∙

As Candice stepped from her car after work, she spotted Jeremy waiting near her apartment. The sight of him with windblown hair and cold, red cheeks made her heart skip a beat. There was something special about Jeremy. And though she knew this, she had treated him shabbily that morning. Why did she lash out at him? It wasn't his fault that Edwardo might be searching for her. Jeremy was nothing like Edwardo, and he deserved better from her. He deserved her honesty.

"Hi, Jeremy," she said in greeting as she walked up to her door. She hated the breathy quality in her voice, but Jeremy didn't seem to notice.

"I don't think we'll have that quiet dinner you planned," Jeremy said, gesturing to the closed apartment door.

"Why wouldn't we?" Candice asked with a frown. Just as she inserted her key in the lock, the door flew open. A giggling young woman stood in the doorway with two others peering around her.

"Who are you, and where is Lindsey?" Candice asked the young woman.

The young woman shrugged. "I don't know. I just got here. You want to come in, or what? You're letting out the heat."

The young woman was saved from Candice's sharp retort as Lindsey swung into view. "Lindsey! What is going on here?" Candice called.

Lindsey pranced over to the doorway. "Candice! I'm just having a few friends over. You don't mind, do you? Come in! We're making fudge in the kitchen, and pizza is on its way."

Candice shook her head, backing away. She was tired of all the parties her roommate had. Lindsey was a nice girl, but she had some growing to do. Candice wasn't sure she had the patience to wait until Lindsey did grow up. "No, thanks, Lindsey. I'll be back later. Just make sure my room is closed."

As Lindsey entered the apartment, Candice turned to Jeremy. "It looks like we need to make different plans. Any ideas?"

Jeremy took Candice's cold hand in his warm one. His fingers engulfed hers, and warmth seeped from his fingers to hers. Candice felt her irritation toward her roommate drain away. "Actually, I do have an idea," he said, "but it doesn't have any room for talking. Are you okay with that?"

Candice thought about how she needed to tell him about Edwardo. She hadn't begun to unearth those feelings from long ago, and she also wasn't sure she was ready to share any of it with Jeremy. She sighed with relief, and gave Jeremy a thankful smile. "Whatever your plan is, it's fine with me."

Jeremy winked at Candice. "Let's go grab a bite to eat, then I'll tell you about my idea."

five

"You have got to be kidding, Jeremy!" Candice said, stunned. When she'd agreed with Jeremy's plans, she'd had no idea what that meant.

Jeremy didn't answer but continued to lead Candice across the snowy park toward the bright lights. He had a firm grip on her hand and practically dragged her through the snow. If Candice could have gotten free, she would have run as fast as she could in the opposite direction. Jeremy must have sensed her reluctance because his grip tightened.

"I can't do this. Come on, Jeremy. Be a nice guy," she pleaded.

Jeremy chuckled deep in his throat. It was a nice sound. "I am a nice guy."

"I know. But you know I can't do this. Why are you being so stubborn?" She tried to dig her heels into the snow but Jeremy wouldn't relent. He tugged on her hand.

"You'll have fun, I promise. Besides, you're the one being stubborn," he teased.

He continued to pull her closer to the bright lights. As their destination came into view, Candice's heart began to pound with trepidation. It was a silly fear she realized, but she was afraid nevertheless. "I really can't ice skate, Jeremy. I've told you this."

"I'm going to teach you. It's fun, and you'll have a great time. There's nothing to worry about."

As they approached the outdoor skating rink, Candice could

see a dozen skaters gliding on the ice. It looked so simple, yet she knew differently. If she got on the ice, it would only mean disaster.

"Jeremy, you really don't know what you're getting yourself into. Besides you have a hurt shoulder. I'm sure I will fall, then I'll drag you down with me, and you'll injure yourself again. This isn't a wise choice, I'm telling you. Why don't we go over to the café and have some nice cocoa and visit," she pleaded.

Jeremy firmly shook his head. "I want to teach you to skate, then maybe sometime you can teach me to ski. I know what I was doing on the mountain resembled a runaway train. Rather embarrassing, I have to admit," he added.

"And now you want me to embarrass myself!" Candice retorted.

"No, I want to teach you something fun. Now stay here while I get us some skates. I don't want to have to tackle you in the snow if you try to escape. Will you stay?"

Candice lifted her chin defiantly. "You wouldn't tackle me!"

"Do you want to press this?" he challenged.

Candice lowered her chin uncertainly. Jeremy nodded victoriously. "Good. I'll be right back. You need a size six?" At Candice's nod, Jeremy hurried over to the booth to rent their skates.

While he was gone, Candice watched the skaters. Two children, probably ages six and eight, were chasing each other around the rink as though they were running in boots. Their parents called after them, laughing and shaking their heads. An older couple skated arm in arm, staring into each other's eyes as their feet moved in perfect harmony. Two teenage girls stayed at the far end of the rink, practicing jumps and spins. Maybe if she hung on to the wall that encircled the rink, she might be able to do this. Maybe.

"Here we go," Jeremy said as he placed a pair of scuffed white skates in Candice's arms. The skates had seen better days. Candice rolled her eyes at Jeremy's smug smile.

Wordlessly she tugged off her boots and shoved her feet into the skates. They were stiff and cold and tighter than her boots. It was an uncomfortable sensation that brought back memories of her last skating disaster. She remembered her parents smiling encouragingly from across the rink as Claire teased her and skated circles around her. In an effort to save her pride, Candice had dashed haphazardly across the rink, only to lose her balance and bruise her chin on the ice. It wasn't a good memory.

Jeremy stilled Candice's hands, drawing her from her reverie. "Stop, Candice. You're doing that all wrong. See here." He motioned to the bunched laces. "They're too loose. You'll give your ankles better support with tight skates. With better support you'll stay upright on the blades." He quickly unlaced Candice's mess and relaced the skates. When he finished, the skates were properly laced and snug. With Jeremy's help, Candice scrambled to her feet. "Easy now. Grab the wall then step onto the ice," he instructed.

Candice followed Jeremy's instructions as he stepped onto the ice and glided effortlessly away from her. He did a quick tour around the rink, slowing to a stop next to Candice. Candice hadn't dared move two inches. "Jeremy, where are my crash helmet and pads? I don't have enough sick leave if I break a bone."

"Take my arm, Candice, with one hand. Let go of the wall. We'll go nice and easy around the rink."

With a steel grip, Candice clutched Jeremy's arm. Slowly she moved forward, her blades sliding smoothly across the ice. "I'm okay, I'm okay, I'm okay," she muttered through clenched teeth. "Hey! This isn't so bad!"

Jeremy laughed. "That's right. Now we're actually going to push away from the wall."

With careful movements, Jeremy led Candice around the rink. She clutched his arm as though he were keeping her from a dangerous precipice. He didn't seem to mind, though she was sure his fingers must tingle from lack of circulation.

After one excruciatingly slow tour around the rink, Candice's confidence began to build. She released Jeremy's arm and struck out on her own. "Just stay close," she ordered Jeremy.

Jeremy stayed in front of Candice, skating backwards. He kept his speed down, measuring his movements with Candice's. It reminded Candice of the older couple with the synchronized steps. She grinned suddenly at Jeremy.

"What's that smile for?" he asked.

"I feel like a bird," she answered. Her arms were outstretched for balance as she scooted her feet across the ice. With a surge of bravery she tried to push off with her left foot and glide on her right. It worked! She then took a cautious nudge with her right foot and glided with her left. "I'm doing it, Jeremy!" With a stronger push of her left foot she propelled herself closer to Jeremy, but it was with more force than she'd anticipated. Her blade caught a rut, and her skate stopped but her body kept moving forward. "Oh, no!"

Jeremy reached forward to stop Candice's fall at the same time she reached out for him. Her flapping arm caught Jeremy in the chin, knocking him off balance. Together they fell in a heap on the ice. "Are you all right, Candice?" Jeremy asked after a stunned moment of silence.

Candice groaned. "At least I didn't land on my chin this time. I think I bruised my cheek."

Jeremy crawled across the ice to Candice. He leaned over to

inspect her reddened cheek, then pressed a gentle kiss against it. "That should make it better. Does it hurt anywhere else?"

Shaking her head, Candice answered, "Only my cheek, but it does feel better."

"Good." Jeremy lowered his head again toward Candice until they were eye to eye. They stared deep into each other's eyes, allowing the world to melt away. "Can I kiss you, Candice Drakeforth?" he whispered.

With a faint nod, Candice felt Jeremy press his warm lips against hers. It was a light, brief kiss, yet never had she experienced anything like it. Jeremy pulled away, looking equally stunned. "I think we'd better end this skating lesson."

Candice shook her head, banishing all the stars from the brief kiss. "I agree, Jeremy, but how am I going to get up? I feel like a clumsy penguin! Maybe I should crawl off the ice." Laughing together, they crawled out of the skating rink.

As Candice put her boots back on and Jeremy returned the skates, she had to smile to herself. Ice skating was fun after all! Her cheek was stinging, and she knew more of her body would ache in the morning, yet she didn't really notice. All she noticed was the full feeling she had in her heart because of Jeremy Braunfeld.

Her lightheartedness faded when she looked across the rink and saw Jeremy's scowl. He had just returned the skates and was coming back for her. Candice jumped to her feet and met him halfway. "What is it, Jeremy? Did I do something?" she asked, her heart beating in dread.

Jeremy looked past Candice to a group of people gathered beyond the rink. "Do you see that guy over there?" Candice looked but didn't notice anyone in particular. "He's been staring at you. Do you know who he is?"

Again Candice scanned the crowd. Her heart began to pound

harder with uncertainty. "I don't see anyone."

Jeremy studied the crowd too. "He must be gone. Come on, let's get out of here." He took Candice's hand, and they left the rink behind. They also left behind their earlier lightheartedness.

Jeremy was quiet the entire drive home. Several times Candice tried to pull him into conversation, but he didn't respond well. Something had been bothering him ever since they left the skating rink.

"Have I done something to upset you?" Candice asked as Jeremy pulled his pickup into the parking lot.

After parking the truck and turning off the ignition, Jeremy turned in his seat to face Candice. She could see a dim outline of his features as he stared intently through the faint light. "It's not you. I just keep thinking about that guy I saw staring at you tonight. I know I've seen him somewhere before. It should be obvious, but I can't bring up a name to match the face, and it's bothering me." He took Candice's hand and gently rubbed her fingers for a moment before continuing. "I've grown to care for you, and I don't like other men staring at you."

"Whoever it was, Jeremy, I don't know him. He doesn't matter. Please don't be angry with me."

Jeremy took Candice's chin in his hand and placed a soft kiss on her lips. "You didn't do anything. Don't think I'm angry with you."

A lump formed in Candice's throat. "I just don't deserve your kindness. I'm afraid I might do or say something that scares you away. Or maybe I'll wake up and realize you were just a dream. If you were gone tomorrow, I wouldn't be surprised."

Shaking his head, Jeremy said, "I don't understand why you're saying these things. Do you honestly believe you might jinx a relationship between us? I don't believe it, and you shouldn't either. I promise you I'll be here tomorrow, and the only way I'm leaving is if you purposely send me away. Do you understand?"

Candice nodded in the darkness. "Okay, Jeremy. Then I'll see you tomorrow?"

"You bet," he answered.

Candice felt some satisfaction with his answer, yet she couldn't help wondering if she might unwittingly send him away. She knew she didn't deserve him, and if he knew her better he would agree.

❧

The next morning Candice slipped out of her bed with a groan of agony. It seemed like every muscle in her body ached from her dive across the skating rink the night before. A glance in the mirror revealed the brilliant shade of purple spreading across her cheek. She wondered if Jeremy would give her cheek another fatherly kiss once he saw it. The thought was pleasant.

As she headed for work on the ski slope, Candice wondered what Jeremy had in store for her that day. He'd promised not to leave and that he would see her. Hopefully he wouldn't make her ice skate again. She'd proven what a klutz on skates she was. Surely he would pick a more sedentary activity.

After getting her assignment for the day, patrolling the south slope, Candice went outside. The sun was shining, and it proved to be a nice day. There was a chance of snow, but the wind wasn't up. She snapped on her skis, grabbed her poles, and headed for the chairlift.

Though the sun was still shining, a dark cloud seemed to come and shadow Candice's day. Something wasn't right. It felt as if someone were watching her. Several times, Candice felt the staring eyes of a stranger, but when she turned to look for him, no one was in sight. Jeremy had mentioned someone watching her the night before, yet she had found no one. Now again, she felt the eyes upon her. Someone unseen. Someone mysterious was watching her.

At an isolated bend on the mountain, an overwhelming sense that someone was watching her sent shivers up Candice's spine. She tucked into a racing position with her knees bent, skis close together, and elbows in. She sped past yards upon yards of the run until she no longer felt as though she were being watched or followed.

At the bottom of the hill, Candice slid to a stop, sending a spray of powdery snow up in a cloud. Without taking a breath, she hurried over to the chair lift and took the line reserved for ski patrol.

"Hey, Candice! Haven't seen you all day! Want to have a coffee break with me later?"

Candice turned her attention to David, the chairlift operator. He was a teenager, just out of high school, and he was one of her many fans. Candice didn't mind his silly flirtations, but she never took him seriously. Today, though, she didn't have the time to cater to his antics. She waved away his suggestion, shaking her head.

"Sorry, David. I need to get back up the mountain. I'll be up there most of the day. Why don't you take out that new girl working in rentals. Isn't her name Julie?"

David's smile was good-natured as he gestured her forward to get on the lift. "She's my second choice. It's too bad my first one didn't pan out. Maybe one of these days you'll see how good I am for you."

Candice didn't have a chance to respond because someone behind her called, "I'm a single! Hold the lift!"

David shook his head. "I can't hold the lift, Buddy. You'll have to wait."

The single skier was determined to get on the lift with Candice. He ignored David's instructions and scooted quickly in next to Candice. Without a second to lose, the chair swung around, hitting them behind the knees, forcing them both to sit. Candice stared in surprise at the skier next to her. She had never seen anyone so anxious to get on the lift. Had he waited about thirty seconds, he would have gotten on the chair behind her.

"See you, David!" Candice called over her shoulder as the chair was whisked into the air. She tucked her ski poles under her legs and reached for the safety bar. The skier next to her also reached for the bar, and together they secured it into place.

Slouching against the cold, padded seat, Candice closed her eyes with a sigh. It was an unusual day. Her thoughts drifted to Jeremy and what his plans might be for the evening. *Hopefully he learned his lesson with the ice skating!* she thought with a smile. She gently rubbed the bruise on her cheek, not minding it at all. Jeremy had kissed her because of it.

"Aren't your boyfriends a little young for you, Candi Kiss?"

Candice was jolted out of her reverie by the intrusive question. The voice brought the familiar sounds of a terrible nightmare. She turned in her seat to stare at the skier, but his hat and goggles hid his face. It didn't matter. She knew who he was. Her eyes narrowed suspiciously as she studied him.

"What do you want, Edwardo?"

Edwardo laughed. "That's some greeting for your fiancé. I thought you would be happy to see me."

Hot frustration raced through Candice's veins as she tried to maintain her temper. Their last encounter jumped into her mind along with all the humiliation and pain she had experienced. "You are not my fiancé. As I recall, you married someone else."

"A poor choice, believe me. And despite what the reporters said, the marriage never actually happened. But that's in the past. Let's talk about our future."

"Our future? We don't have a future! You made your choice when you ridiculed me in front of so many people. I've moved on, and my life is very different now."

Edwardo smirked at Candice. "Yes, I see what a success you've made of your life. Holed up in this mountain hide-away. You're wasting your talents. All you do is baby-sit these amateur skiers. Don't you miss the cameras, costumes, and parties? Don't you miss the money?"

Candice emphatically shook her head. "No! I don't miss anything about that life. It was all a bad nightmare that I'm still ashamed of. I want nothing to do with that time, and having you here only brings back those terrible memories."

Edwardo sat back and put his arm behind Candice. Nothing she said seemed to penetrate his ego. "You could show me a little warmth since I had to track you down in this sub-zero peasant village. You weren't easy to find, you know."

"Were you the one to contact my sister and my boss? Did you follow me this morning?"

Edwardo grinned. "Guilty. You took off like a scared rabbit. It was quite a sight."

Before Candice could retort, she noticed they were nearing the end of the lift. Without comment she raised the safety bar and scooted to the edge of the chair. She hoped Edwardo had some skiing ability so he wouldn't crash into her as they descended from the lift. She smoothly rose from the chair and skied away from Edwardo as fast as she could. Behind her she could hear him calling.

"We're not done with this, Candi. It's only beginning!"

six

"I can't believe he's here," Candice mumbled to herself all the way home. Ever since Edwardo had humiliated her, or rather ever since she'd humiliated herself at that audition, Candice had wondered what she would say if she ever saw Edwardo again. She'd never imagined she would actually hold a civilized conversation with him. Not that he deserved anything civilized. The way he had treated her, he deserved a thrashing, but she didn't give it to him. She had been civilized. She had been a lot more controlled than she felt at the moment.

"Why is he here?" Candice moaned. Jeremy's image floated through her mind. Jeremy was a nice guy. He was someone she could easily fall in love with and live happily ever after. Then Edwardo had to show up. Just the sight of him made her pulse pick up speed and sent her emotions into turmoil. She couldn't still be in love with him, could she? She stiffened at the thought. That was impossible. He was a horrible, self-serving man. Besides, how could she be attracted to Jeremy if she was still in love with Edwardo? No, that wasn't possible.

Just as Candice entered her apartment, the telephone started ringing. She raced to pick up the receiver before the answering machine turned on.

"Hello?" she answered, out of breath. She hoped it wasn't Edwardo. Maybe she should have let the machine get the call.

"Hey, Beautiful! How was your day?"

Candice relaxed at the sound of the warm deep voice. "Jeremy!"

"I was wondering if you want to come see the condos. It's dark, but I have a pretty powerful flashlight. And I promise if you hang onto me, nothing will happen."

"That's an offer I can't refuse. When can I expect you?"

After settling on a time, Candice hurried to her bedroom to get ready. She took extra pains with her appearance. After the previous night's skating disaster, she didn't want him to see her as a clumsy waif. The purple bruise on her cheek was evidence of her lack of grace, and she couldn't cover it with any amount of makeup. Around Jeremy she behaved nothing like she normally did. First she was plowed over by the sled, and then she crashed on the ice, but that had been his fault. She had warned Jeremy she was a disaster on skates. Still, she wasn't normally accident-prone. Men used to see her as a sophisticated, drop-dead actress with style and finesse, not as a bruised maniac. She hoped Jeremy didn't see her either way. She wanted something in the middle. She wanted him to think of her as lovely. She carefully brushed out her hair and left it hanging past her shoulders. She applied just a dab of makeup. She now hated all the "artificial beauty" as her sister Claire called it. After pulling on a pair of slacks and a matching sweater, she felt ready for her date. As she tied her shoes, the doorbell rang.

"He's earlier than he said," Candice noted, glancing at the clock. With a shrug she hurried to the door and threw it wide. "Hi, Jeremy!"

"Not quite, Candi Kiss." Edwardo stood in the doorway. The expression on his handsome face was smug. Candice sucked in her breath at the sight of him. He still made her heart race with the sound of her name on his lips. How many women did he have the same effect on?

Edwardo's eyes narrowed. "So who's Jeremy?" he asked.

"He's a guy I've been going out with. And I don't really see how he's any of your concern. You gave up your rights long ago, Edwardo."

Candice's cold delivery didn't cause Edwardo's smug grin to slip an inch. He gave her body a slow perusal. At one time his appreciation would have been welcome, but now it infuriated her. She wanted to slap his smug face and send him packing, yet her arms felt glued to her sides and the sharp retort was trapped on her weighted tongue.

"You still look good, Candi Kiss. Time has done you many favors."

His bold appraisal finally loosened Candice's tongue. "Why are you here?" she asked abruptly.

Edwardo reached out and brushed away a strand of Candice's hair. "I just wanted to see how you were doing," he said softly. "You've let your hair grow. I always said you would look pretty with long hair."

Candice backed away from his touch. "Don't you think it's a little late to look in on me? You could have checked a few years ago."

Edwardo ignored the brush-off and took a step closer. "Can't we just leave the past in the past and start over here?"

Candice's mouth went dry as Edwardo moved even closer. She couldn't have spoken had she tried.

"Sometimes the past needs to be dealt with."

Candice glanced around Edwardo to see Jeremy walking up the path. He stuck out his hand to shake Edwardo's. "I'm Jeremy Braunfeld."

Edwardo took a quick step away from Candice, clearly annoyed by Jeremy's interruption. Jeremy didn't look too pleased either. "And I'm Edwardo Estanza, Candi's fiancé."

Candice cringed when Jeremy turned in surprise toward

her. Indignant, Candice stamped her foot. "That's not true, Edwardo. You are not my fiancé, and we have nothing more to say." She turned her attention to Jeremy as she pulled the door shut behind her and stepped around Edwardo.

"Are you ready to go?" She didn't miss the nonverbal yet stormy communication that passed between the two men. Jeremy moved closer to Candice and put his arm around her shoulders.

"If you're all done here, the truck is still running," he said, not taking his gaze from Edwardo.

Without a backward glance Candice walked with Jeremy to his waiting pickup. He handed her into the passenger seat before circling around to the driver's side. Wordlessly, he pulled from the parking lot and headed toward the new construction site.

"I'm sorry about that, Jeremy. I don't know why Edwardo thinks I'm his fiancée because I'm not. The relationship ended a long time ago."

Jeremy didn't answer right away. "I have to admit I didn't like finding him on your doorstep. I've never found myself to be a jealous man, but I can't help myself when it comes to you. I feel very possessive," he said quietly.

"If it's any consolation, I didn't like finding him on my doorstep either. For some reason he has decided to intrude in my life, and I don't know why."

"Remember when we were at the skating rink last night and I said there was a guy staring at you? He was the guy."

"I'm sorry, Jeremy." Candice placed her hand on his arm. "I hope you won't stop coming around because of him. I'm sure that's exactly what he wants."

"Candice, as long as you're not interested in Edwardo, I don't care what he does. He won't keep me from seeing you.

You're very special to me, and I intend to spend every possible minute I have with you. So let's not talk about him anymore. We're at the condos, and I want you to enjoy yourself."

"Okay, Jeremy. I'll try not to think about him anymore." Candice pushed her thoughts of Edwardo to the back of her mind, but it wasn't easy to keep them there. Somehow she felt guilty for his intrusion.

As Candice reached for the door handle, Jeremy stopped her.

"Wait, I have something for you." He reached behind the seat and pulled out a medium-sized gift bag.

"What is this?"

Jeremy grinned but didn't answer, so Candice reached into the bag. She laughed when she pulled out the furry stuffed animal.

"It's a penguin!" She hugged it to her. "Jeremy, it's perfect."

"I wanted you to remember our date last night, and I thought this was the best way." He gingerly cupped her chin in his hand and kissed her.

"I think we better go see the condo," he whispered after a moment. Candice couldn't agree more. His kisses were a little too potent.

Jeremy helped Candice out of the truck and led her along a snowy path to the newly constructed condominiums. The three buildings, each with four units, were all at a different point of completion.

"Come see the farthest one. It is the closest to being finished."

Candice followed Jeremy to the condominium. He helped her step up through the framed doorway. He clicked on his flashlight and aimed the beam through the bare rooms.

"Over there is the kitchen, and to the left is the living room," Jeremy explained.

Taking Jeremy's hand, Candice followed him through the

rooms. Sheetrock hadn't been put on the walls, so it was difficult to imagine what the finished product would look like.

"Will it have a fireplace? After a long day on the slopes, there's nothing like a warm fire."

"It will have a gas fireplace; less mess and more efficient. It will be right over there. Now here's what I wanted to show you." Jeremy led Candice across the spacious living room to the back wall where a large window would be placed. "Look out there," he instructed.

Candice peered through the darkness at a small frozen lake. The condominiums encircled one side of the lake. Tall pine trees nestled against the other side. It was a cozy setting that would be appealing in both winter and summer months. Candice could imagine sitting on a back deck and reading a book, or floating along in a canoe.

"It's like a postcard, Jeremy. This is a lovely spot for a home."

Jeremy smiled down at her. "It's also a good pond for ice skating."

"Oh, no! No more ice skating for me!"

Jeremy placed a quick peck on Candice's lips. "Give me some time, my little penguin. I'll change your mind."

&

After saying goodnight to Jeremy later that evening, Candice let herself into her apartment. She really liked Jeremy. Whenever she was with him she felt totally at ease. God had blessed her with a really good friend, and maybe with time it might develop into something more. The thought made her catch her breath.

"Please, Lord, let it be something more," she whispered.

"How was your date?"

Candice whirled to find Edwardo sitting on her sofa. He

held a mug of coffee in one hand and her TV remote in the other.

"How did you get in here?"

"When I explained who I was to your roommate, she was more than happy to let me in. Unfortunately she couldn't stay and entertain me because she had a date. So I've been left to amuse myself." He studied Candice's flushed cheeks and sparkling eyes. "Nice penguin," he muttered dryly, pointing at the stuffed animal in Candice's arms.

Candice sighed, silently praying for patience and a level head. She didn't want Edwardo in her life again. He represented so much pain. And she was afraid to be alone with him. She was afraid to find out she might still care for him. "Please, Edwardo, tell me why you're here."

Edwardo flashed Candice his hundred-watt smile that at one time had made jelly of her legs and melted her resolve. Now she felt nothing. Maybe, since his old charms didn't work, she didn't love him after all.

"You're too far away from me. Come sit here, and we'll talk," Edwardo instructed, patting the sofa next to him.

Candice walked from the doorway and sat in the chair across from Edwardo. She wasn't about to be within his reach. His smile might not affect her, but there was no telling what his touch could do, and she didn't want him to find her weaknesses.

"So you're being stubborn—"

"Cautious, not stubborn," Candice interjected.

Edwardo shrugged. "I can work with that. Now put down that stupid doll, Candi. You're not a child needing toys."

Candice reluctantly set the penguin at her feet. She resented the way Edwardo ordered her around. She threw him a scathing look, daring him to say anything else.

"The reason I've come is because I want to patch things up between us. We had it so good, and I want those good times back. You and I were like milk and honey, roses and chocolate, snowstorms and cocoa. We went together."

"Please," Candice held up her hand to stop his ardent analogies. "No more. I think we both know you're feeding me a line. Tell me why you're really here, and it better be the truth."

Scooting to the edge of his seat, Edwardo tried another of his appealing looks. Wide, bottomless black eyes stared at her beseechingly. "I have been telling you the truth, but you're right. I have another reason. I'm getting ready to shoot a film, and there is a part in it that is perfect for you. The role calls for someone who can act but also ski. They want to shoot the film at this resort, and we already have the owners halfway convinced. I know if you come on board with the project, the owners will let it fly. It will be good publicity for the resort to have one of their employees in a lead role. What do you think?"

All the horrors of the past flooded over Candice. She could picture herself standing on the stage with not one line of the words she had worked so hard to learn passing through her mind. It had been the worst moment to get stage fright. She'd stared in anguish at all the people waiting for her to begin. And then the smirking began. Some chuckled. A few shook their heads. The laughter had been unbearable. How could he laugh at her? He was supposed to love her!

Shaking with the memories, Candice jumped to her feet. "No! Get out of my house, Edwardo. I will not be laughed at again." A knot formed in her throat, and she had to keep the tears of anger and humiliation from showing themselves. "Get out!"

Rising slowly to his feet, Edwardo interjected, "Candi,

Sweetheart, nobody is laughing at you. Don't be so sensitive. This is your big chance to get your career back on track. It's your chance to redeem yourself with the acting community. Don't throw this chance away."

"Get out!" Candice preceded Edwardo to the door and held it wide open for him.

Edwardo slowly followed, shaking his head. "I won't take this as your final answer. We'll talk some more after you've had a night to think about it." Before she could protest, Edwardo pulled her into his arms and placed a quick kiss on her lips. "We will talk about us too when you're calm. Good night, Candi Kiss."

Candice slammed the door after Edwardo. He had nerve to come asking her for favors. Shaking with emotion, Candice went back to her chair and sat. She pulled the fluffy penguin onto her lap and buried her face in its softness. She couldn't even bring herself to look at her sofa where Edwardo had been moments earlier. He infuriated her. His presence brought to life all the things that she'd believed were buried in her past.

Something else bothered her too, and it was difficult to admit. His offer of a movie role struck a chord deep inside her. She didn't want to believe that she missed acting. That part of her life was over, and she was glad to be separated from it. Yet given a chance to act again, would she do it? Perhaps she really did want to get back into acting.

"Lord, help me to know what to do. I don't want to deal with any of this. First Jeremy came into my life. His forgiveness of me has turned into something wonderful. I enjoy his company so much. Then Edwardo shows up. I don't see how that situation can turn into anything wonderful. Why, all of a sudden, is my past being thrown in my face? What am I supposed to learn from this? I don't want to deal with these things. That's why I left acting and moved to these isolated mountains. Please, Lord, help me to be free from my past."

After praying Candice felt a little better, but she still didn't have any answers. She knew for a fact she didn't want to be in the movie. Convincing Edwardo of that wouldn't be easy. She remembered how stubborn and pushy he was when he set his heart on something. She hoped she wouldn't react the way she used to, by giving in to his wishes.

æ

The next morning Candice was determined to avoid all contact with Edwardo so she got up early, set the answering machine to take all calls, and told her roommate that she didn't want to see Edwardo. Lindsey didn't understand Candice's reluctance to see that "gorgeous movie star," but she accepted Candice's wishes. Before Edwardo could show up and corner her in her own home, Candice packed a picnic lunch for two in her backpack, loaded up her cross-country ski equipment, and headed over to Jeremy's construction site.

She found Jeremy standing in the doorway of one of the condos. He had a yellow hard hat on his head and a clipboard in his hands. He seemed to be having a heated discussion with one of the workers. Candice hoped she hadn't picked a bad time to come by. As she cautiously approached Jeremy, he became aware of her presence. His frown evaporated into a wide grin as he watched her come near.

"I thought you were working today," he called.

"I decided to take the day off. If I can persuade you to leave with me, I have a fun-filled day planned for us. What do you say?"

"I think your plan is the answer to my problem. Give me a few minutes, will you?" Candice watched as Jeremy turned back to the worker. The conversation was a lot calmer than earlier, and the two men parted with a handshake.

Candice watched Jeremy walk across the cluttered lot toward her. She was again struck by how handsome he was. Why had she never noticed him the first time they met? The answer immediately came to mind. Edwardo. Edwardo had clouded everything she saw, and he was back trying to gain the same results.

"What's the frown for?" Jeremy asked as he came to a stop in front of her. He slowly traced the frown lines around her mouth with his finger. His touch was cool but not unwelcome. "It must be serious to make you so upset."

Giving herself a good mental shake, Candice tried to laugh off his concern. "It's nothing, really. I don't want to talk about it. How is your shoulder feeling?"

"Fine." Jeremy continued to study her face, not missing any of the emotions that flashed by on wide-screen. "I can tell you're upset about something. You'll feel better if you talk it out."

"I guess my acting skills are slipping if you can read me that well." Candice forced a laugh, but Jeremy wasn't fooled. "Let's talk about it later, okay? I don't want to think about him anymore." She circled her car and slid behind the wheel. Jeremy took the cue and let himself in on the passenger side.

He wasn't about to let the conversation drop. "Him. Him, as in Edwardo Estanza?"

"Yes, him. He told me why he's here. He wants me to take a part in a movie." Her grip tightened on the wheel. She reached for the key and started the car.

Jeremy studied Candice's profile as she drove. "How do you feel about it?"

"I'm not sure. I've always liked acting. I was doing fairly well when everything came crashing down. This might be a chance to start again." Her words so closely echoed Edwardo's that Candice cringed. "But I don't think I'll do it," she finished.

"Are you sure? You just said you enjoyed acting. You could give it a try again and see how it goes. If it doesn't work out that well, then don't continue. I remember how you were in front of those cameras. You were amazing."

Candice shook her head. "It doesn't work that way. I can't just quit in the middle of filming. And it's not the acting that I'm afraid of; it's the lifestyle that goes along with it. I am so ashamed of the way I behaved. I don't want to ever be that person again. I won't do this film."

"Just because you're acting in a movie doesn't mean you have to behave in an unchristian way. The two don't have to go hand in hand. The Lord will be your strength."

"Jeremy, can we stop talking about this? I want to have a fun day with you. I don't want to think about Edwardo or this movie. I'd rather think about cross-country skiing."

Candice drove to a sports rental shop, and they quickly outfitted Jeremy with everything he would need for the day. She then took him to a remote area outside of town that had great cross-country paths through the hills.

The snowy area was beautiful with the sun reflecting off the snow. Little sparkles of light glistened on the untouched meadow. It looked like millions of diamonds sparkling in the sunlight. Even the well-used path glistened welcomingly. The path started at the parking lot and led straight into the woods.

"I'm not going to get eaten by a bear, am I?" Jeremy joked as he fastened on his skis. The skis were long and narrower than the downhill skis. And instead of wearing the large cumbersome downhill boots, he wore lightweight shoes that fastened into the skis' bindings.

"Nope, no bears. But we might see a hungry mountain

lion." At Jeremy's startled glance, Candice quickly added, "Actually, we'll probably see little bunnies and maybe a chipmunk. And if we're really quiet we might even see a deer. And you'll see lots of trees and snow. The mountain lions don't like to come around noisy people."

"Okay, I get the idea. And guess what? I've done this before so you won't have to rescue me. But you go first."

"If you insist," Candice answered. She pulled on her gloves and slipped on sunglasses. She then scooted onto the path, her skis slipping into the well-worn grooves made by many previous skiers. She struck out, sliding her right ski forward and reaching with her left pole, then reversing by sliding her left ski forward and reaching with her right pole. The sound was gentle and rhythmic, echoing in the quiet valley. She could hear Jeremy following her a few feet behind.

Soon they'd traveled across the bright meadow and into the shadows of the forest. It was cooler in the midst of the trees. Light filtered down through the branches but didn't provide much warmth. Candice's breath came out in frequent white puffs. She led Jeremy up small inclines and down gentle hills, following the curving path. Though the air was cool to breathe, the exercise made Candice warm. It was hard work maintaining the sliding rhythm. While downhill skiing was exhilarating, cross-country skiing was a total body workout. What made all the hard work rewarding was the peacefulness. The only sounds were the occasional bird calls or the sound of snow falling from branches. The noise of skis sliding across the snow was almost deafening in the quiet.

After thirty minutes on the path Candice called over her shoulder, "Ready for a break?"

"Anytime is fine," Jeremy answered back.

Candice followed the path out of the trees into a small

clearing where backpackers camped in the summer. A picnic table sat in the middle of the clearing, warmed by the sunlight. It was one of Candice's favorite picnic spots.

"Hey, this looks great," Jeremy said as he came to a stop next to Candice.

"How is your shoulder feeling?" Candice asked. She hoped she hadn't pushed him to do too much too soon.

Jeremy wiped beads of perspiration from his forehead. "It's a little sore, but the exercise is probably good for it. I think I was ready for a break, though."

"Good. Let's eat."

They unfastened their skis and leaned them against a tree. Holding hands, Jeremy led Candice to the picnic table. Many inches of snow had fallen since the last skiers had used the table, so getting to it wasn't easy. They both sank to their knees in the soft powdery snow.

"This is more of a workout than the skiing!" As Jeremy tried to take another step in the deep snow, he lost his balance and fell face first in the snow, pulling Candice down with him.

"Hey! Next time you fall, let go of my hand!" Candice laughed. She half crawled, half stumbled, trying to regain her footing. Cold snow covered her face and melted on her neck.

"I think I lost my glove," Jeremy groaned. He held up his bare hand. Candice groaned too. It would be hard to find his glove in all that powder. Together they dug in the snow where Jeremy had fallen. Fine snow flew into the air as they thrashed about.

"I found it!" Candice announced as she held up his blue glove.

"Good! My fingers were beginning to freeze." He took the glove and shoved his hand into it. "And I think you deserve a kiss for finding it for me." Jeremy leaned toward Candice, but she pushed him away.

"Oh, no, you don't! I don't want to fall in this stuff again!"

Finally, they made it to the picnic table and devoured the sandwiches Candice had brought. It was a little early for lunch, but neither minded. They munched on apples and chips, then washed it all down with small bottles of juice.

"Candice, if you don't accept the movie part, do you plan to stay here working for the resort?"

"Of course. Why?"

Jeremy hesitated as though considering his words. "Well, I know we haven't known each other long, but I enjoy being with you so much. I have two months left here. At least that's what the projected finish date is for the condos. Then I have another job lined up in Colorado Springs. Do you spend your summers up here too?"

"No, I leave the mountains to go stay with my sister and her husband."

"I don't think I'm saying this very well, and maybe I'm being presumptuous, but I don't want our relationship to end when my project ends. Maybe we can work something out so we can stay near each other."

Candice wasn't sure what Jeremy was implying. She didn't want the relationship to end, either. Was he suggesting she move to Colorado Springs with him? "Two months is still plenty of time. Why don't we figure it out then?"

Jeremy nodded, but Candice could tell he wanted to say more. She didn't think either of them was ready for it though.

"Yes, Candice, you're right. We'll consider it then. Ready to get back on the skis?"

seven

Candice stared impatiently at Edwardo leaning against her kitchen counter. She didn't want him in her home, especially when her roommate wasn't there, but Edwardo had insisted.

"Have you thought about my offer?"

Candice studied Edwardo. He seemed less sure of himself as he waited for her answer. It was strange to see him dressed casually in jeans and a T-shirt. He normally thought casual meant slacks and a dress shirt. "If you don't take the part, we might lose the funding for the film."

Candice crossed her arms over her chest. "I've thought about your offer, but I'm not ready to agree to anything yet. To be honest with you, I really don't like the idea of being in a movie."

Edwardo nodded but didn't comment. "Now what about my other offer? What do you think about that?"

"What other offer? I don't know what you're talking about."

"Us. I want us to get back together." He stuffed his hands deep into his pockets as he watched her expressions. "Wait. Before you answer I want to give you something." He pulled his hand out of his pocket and handed her a small box. "I think you'll remember this. You left it with my agent."

Candice refused to take the box Edwardo held out to her. She knew what was in it, and she didn't want any part of it. She took a step back. "There is no us, Edwardo. Please put that back in your pocket. I won't take it."

Despite Candice's protests, Edwardo opened the box. Inside

was a two-karat diamond encircled with rubies. It was a beautiful ring that Candice had been proud to wear at one time. Now the sight of it repulsed her. She felt engulfed with shame and disgust. "Put it away, Edwardo," she whispered.

"Remember the good times, Candi Kiss? We were good together. Think about Mexico. Hot nights, sandy beach, the cool ocean breeze blowing on us as we walked hand in hand."

"Stop it, Edwardo."

"Remember that party in Reno? I bet if we had been in Vegas we would have gotten married."

Candice took another step back as Edwardo stepped toward her. "No, Edwardo. Don't do this. It has been over for a long time." She bumped into the counter as she backed away. There was no place for her to go.

Edwardo ignored her protests as he stepped closer, leaving only inches between them. Slowly he pulled her toward him with one hand while cupping her face in his other hand.

Candice wanted to move, to run far away, but she couldn't. She was frozen in place, and time stopped. The years and the pain dropped away with his touch. His lips covered hers in a possessive kiss.

While his touch was familiar, it was no longer welcome. Candice felt like she was sinking in a pit of shame, and there was no one to throw her a lifeline. She felt limp and powerless in Edwardo's arms, and she hated it. Jeremy's words suddenly entered her mind, filling her with new resolve: "God will be your strength." Yes! God was her strength. He was her lifeline. Even Edwardo could not stand against that. Calling on the strength that God promised, Candice was able to push Edwardo away from her.

"Don't ever do that again! I am not your woman, Edwardo, and I am not available at your beck and call. You may not take such liberties with me again."

Edwardo backed away, surprised by her sudden rejection of his affections. He wordlessly stared at her as though he had never seen her. Candice crossed her arms over her chest, breaking Edwardo's scrutiny. He snapped the ring box shut and set it on the kitchen table. "I'll talk to you later, Candi. I know this is sudden. I'll give you all the time you need to make the right decision."

As Edwardo left, quietly closing the door behind him, Candice sagged against the wall with relief. She couldn't believe the effect Edwardo still had on her, and worse, she knew he had even greater resources of charm to draw on if he decided to.

She needed to talk to someone about the situation. She felt like she was drifting on a sea of confusion and needed someone to help clear the way. Her roommate was sweet and tried to be understanding, but she was young and had stars in her eyes where Edwardo was concerned. Another option was her parents in Montana, but they were so far away that she didn't want to concern them. Claire had her hands full with Rick and planning for the baby. She didn't need to hear about Candice's troubles with men.

Picking up the telephone, she quickly dialed Jeremy's number. He answered on the second ring.

"Are you all right, Candice? You sound like something's bothering you."

Candice gripped the phone tighter. "No, I'm not all right. I really need someone to talk to. Can I meet you somewhere? How about our little café?"

"I'll be there in ten minutes."

Thankfully the little café wasn't crowded when Candice arrived. She didn't want to wait for an available table or have someone overhear their conversation. She chose a table for two in the far corner of the restaurant. She didn't even have time to remove her coat before Jeremy arrived.

"What's going on?" he asked as he took off his coat and gloves. He brushed the snow from his hair and sat across the table from Candice.

Candice suddenly felt tongue-tied as she stared back at Jeremy. How could she tell him that she'd kissed her ex-fiancé and that Edwardo was pressuring her to get back together with him? What she wanted to say was that she was confused by her feelings, but deep down in her heart she felt that she was falling in love with Jeremy. And that knowledge was both exciting and scary. She was scared of messing up the one relationship that could mean more than anything to her. She was afraid to love Jeremy on the chance that he didn't return her feelings. And more than anything, she didn't feel she deserved the love of a man as fine as Jeremy.

"I can see a million emotions playing across your face," Jeremy stated. "What aren't you telling me? Does it have to do with us? If you need to take a step back, I understand."

What does that mean? Candice wondered. It sounded like Jeremy wanted to take a step back in their relationship. Boy, was she glad she hadn't blurted out that she loved him! And what did she know about love anyway? She wasn't sure if she was still in love with Edwardo.

"I just met with Edwardo. He gave me this." Candice set the box containing the engagement ring on the table. Jeremy opened the box, letting out a low whistle. He held the ring up to the light where the large diamond glittered brilliantly.

"What does this mean?" he asked slowly.

"It means nothing as far as I'm concerned. It's my old engagement ring. He's pressuring me to take it back, but I don't want it." After a moment she added, "He kissed me."

"He kissed you," Jeremy repeated, his voice sounding flat. "I'm not sure why you're telling me all this. Like I said, we can take a step back from the relationship if you want."

Candice shook her head. "No, Jeremy! It's not what I want. I feel awful when I'm around Edwardo. And his kiss left me feeling so ashamed. I don't know why he chose now to come back into my life. He's trying to ruin everything."

"And you're telling me all this because. . . ?"

"Because I don't want you to think I'm seeing someone behind your back. I'm not. I'm just confused, and I'm having a hard time dealing with all this."

Jeremy stuck the ring back in its box and slid it across the table to Candice. "The last thing I want is you feeling confused about me. I'm very certain of my feelings for you, but I'm not going to pressure you. It seems to me that you have some things in your past that still need to be resolved before you can move forward."

"How do I move forward, Jeremy? How do I get around all these things when they keep popping up? I thought I had dealt with them. I was fine. Then Edwardo showed up, and everything was turned upside down."

"I think it's something you're going to have to work out with God's help. You need to ask Him to show you what needs to be confronted. When He shows you, and He will, you need to have courage to face those things. Then they will finally be laid to rest. If you don't do this, you can expect things to always pop up unexpectedly, and they will turn your world upside down again and again."

"While I'm trying to deal with all this, what about us, Jeremy? Where will you be?"

"I'll be here for you, don't worry. I'll support you as well as any friend could."

A waitress approached their table, noting the somber mood of the couple. "Are you ready to order? Can I get you anything to drink?" she asked.

"Two coffees," Jeremy requested while looking for Candice's approval. She nodded. "I think that will be all." The waitress hurried away to fill their order.

"I think I can do this, even though I'm not sure what exactly I'm going to do," Candice said.

The waitress returned with two steaming mugs of coffee and placed them on the table. "Holler if you need anything else," she said, turning her attention to some customers who had just entered.

"I think we need to make a toast," Jeremy suggested, raising his mug.

Candice followed his example and raised her own. "What are we toasting?"

"To your freedom, Candice. Only through God's extreme grace will you find it."

Tapping Jeremy's mug with hers, Candice echoed, "To freedom." She wondered what price that freedom would cost her.

ஃ

Candice returned to her apartment to find Edwardo waiting outside her front door. He looked cold, huddled in his thick jacket. His chin was tucked to his chest, and he pressed his back against the door.

"Doesn't it ever stop snowing here?" he complained as Candice approached.

"Do you always show up uninvited on my doorstep?" Candice returned. She moved past him and unlocked the door.

"You must have said something unflattering about me to your roommate because she wouldn't even let me in to wait for you," he accused as he followed her inside.

"I told her not to let you in again because I don't like to come home to unexpected guests. It doesn't matter to me if you're a movie star or the president. It's not right. But I'm glad you stopped by."

Edwardo brightened with her words. "You are?"

"Yes," she turned to him and held out the engagement ring. "You forgot to take this with you."

Edwardo's brightness dissolved. "Let's talk about the movie then. I've been talking with the owners, and they are adamant about having you in the film. Will you reconsider? You would be a perfect fit for the part. And I've seen you ski. You're good enough to do stunts."

"How big of a part is it?"

"It's a major supporting role. It's an action film with a little mystery too. And we didn't forget the romance to keep the ladies in the audience."

"What about a contract?"

"Of course there's a contract. You name your terms, and I'll have them met as best I can. Does this mean you'll do it?" He crossed the room and tried to pull her into his arms.

Candice resisted his embrace. "I don't have an agent anymore, as you probably realize. But I'm not an idiot, Edwardo. I'm not going to be a part of any movie until I get the contract and see a script. I'll give you my answer after I've had a chance to look over the contract."

Edwardo seemed uncomfortable. "I don't see why you're getting hung up on a contract."

Candice planted her fists on her hips. "No contract, no Candice Drakeforth," she answered stiffly.

"Even if it's a Bryan Wright film?"

Candice's stubbornness wavered. "Bryan Wright? You've

got to be joking. How did you ever meet Bryan Wright? I don't believe you, Edwardo."

Edwardo shook his head. "No! I met Bryan Wright at a party, and we just clicked. He told me about this project he's getting ready to do, and I must have impressed him. He specifically asked for you too."

Candice stared incredulously at Edwardo. Bryan Wright? He was the biggest and hottest producer of the decade. At one time Candice would have done anything to star in one of his films. He turned unknown actresses into household names. "How can I believe you're telling the truth?"

Edwardo pulled a folded letter from his pocket. "Read this. It should be proof enough."

Candice opened the letter and scanned the contents. The letter had Bryan Wright's office heading and his bold signature at the bottom. She noticed her name in the body of the letter. "It says here he wants me in the film. It's really Bryan Wright?" she asked in awe.

"The Bryan Wright."

"I guess I'll do it then. I can't believe I'm going to be in a Bryan Wright film."

Edwardo looked as though he wanted to leap and whoop with joy. "I'll get things started. You'll receive a copy of the script in a few days, along with the contract. And within the week, all the equipment will be rolling into town. It'll be good, you'll see, Candi."

As the door closed, Candice answered, "I hope so. Please, Lord, let this be the way." Her voice echoed through the room sounding uncertain and hopeless.

eight

Candice stood shivering at the top of the steep hill. The intermediate run stretching out in front of her had been blocked off from use so the movie could be filmed without interruption. Her body felt frozen as she waited for the director to give her instructions. The sun was bright, but cold gusts of wind blasted the crew. Edwardo stood off to the side, whispering in the ear of his makeup girl.

"Typical," Candice muttered as the girl giggled over something Edwardo said. It didn't really matter to her what Edwardo did and who he saw. She was relieved when she didn't feel even a twinge of jealousy at the sight of him with another woman. When they were engaged, Edwardo would flirt with other women just to infuriate Candice. She fell for it every time, often making a scene. This time, instead of marching over to the woman and ridiculing her in public, Candice merely turned her head.

The film director frowned in Edwardo's direction. "Hey, Estanza! Send your girlfriend away so we can get started. The good light won't last all afternoon. I don't want to have to change locations just because you were fooling around!"

Edwardo shrugged sheepishly as the young woman hurried away, slipping in the snow with her designer shoes. Candice wondered why she hadn't seen through him when she had been engaged to him. He was behaving in the same immature way. Any fool would have seen him for what he truly was. And that's exactly what she had been. A fool. Perhaps she was still a fool since she had agreed to this film. She felt exasperated with Edwardo but not furious. She reserved that emotion for herself. Red hot anger over her repeated stupidity rolled around in the pit of her stomach. She tried to mask her emotions; after all she was an actress again. She didn't want anyone else knowing of the volatile temper that raged within her at the moment. If nothing else, searching for that freedom Jeremy described was proving one thing. She didn't have peace. And she wasn't sure making movies was the way to get it. The whole scenario made her feel worse. Perhaps she'd enjoyed making movies at one time, but shivering at the top of the mountain as she waited for instructions, Candice was sure of one thing: She no longer liked making movies.

"All right, Candi. You're going to ski down the hill in an S-shaped pattern. Make sure you're at the left side of the slope when you near the second camera crew. At that point, look over your left shoulder. It's a determined look, not fearful. Remember you're a woman in control of the situation no matter who is chasing you."

Candice found that ironic. Yes, she was in control. At least that's how she appeared. She snapped her feet into the bindings and reached for her poles, which were planted in the snow next to her.

"Remember to pull down the goggles," the director reminded her. When Candice was ready to begin, he yelled, "Ready! Action!"

Candice took off down the steep slope with her knees bent, skis close, and poles tucked into her side. She knew that a cameraman at the top of the hill was filming her descent. She followed the imaginary line that formed the wide S down the slope. Just as she neared the second camera crew, she straightened slightly, pursed her lips, and looked over her shoulder. Of course no one was following her, though dozens of people were watching her every move. Later they would blend different shots, and it would appear that she was being chased down the hill.

Next they filmed various takes of Candice zipping over a bumpy trail through the trees. She didn't like "tree bashing"— it wasn't safe because the trails were narrow, sometimes just a foot wide, and very unpredictable. Branches hung low, the dips were deep, and trees were snug against the narrow trail. Over and over the director demanded Candice redo the shot. And each time she had to say a quick prayer for safety. She didn't want to hit a tree or fly off the trail and break her leg, which was possible at the high speed they wanted her to take the trail. If that happened, she would not only be out of the movie, but she would also be out of her job for the rest of the season.

Between shots Candice was able to sit with a blanket tucked up to her chin and a hot bottle between her feet. The woman who served as her assistant gave Candice steaming coffee from a thermos.

"Do you know what's up next?" Candice asked her assistant. The young woman shook her head as she retouched Candice's makeup that seemed to melt away with her perspiration. Candice noticed that her assistant was very attractive. Her blond hair was similar to Candice's, as were her expressive green eyes. They could have passed for sisters.

"Is Bryan Wright coming today?" Candice asked. "I wouldn't blame him if he stayed off the mountain. It's freezing." Still Candice's assistant didn't comment.

Candice made another attempt to get the young woman to talk. "Have you been doing this long? You seem to know exactly what I need before I can think of it. I wouldn't have thought of bringing a blanket up the mountain."

The woman smiled faintly. "It's my job to think of those things." Candice briefly turned her attention to where they filmed Edwardo's skiing parts. His ability was laughable, but he made up for his mistakes with his flash and zeal. Slowly he made it halfway down the hill. Candice wondered if they would have to speed up the film to make him appear to be going faster.

Tired of watching Edwardo, Candice turned her attention back to her assistant. "Tell me your name. I don't think we've ever met."

"I'm Andrea Crown. And no, we've never officially met, but you're quite famous. I always wondered what it would be like to work with you."

A trace of apprehension crept into Candice's heart. "I'm not famous anymore. Now I'm just a member of ski patrol at this resort. A regular person," she added.

"You are a lot different to work with than I thought. My friend worked with you down in Mexico. She said it was an experience she will never forget."

Candice briefly closed her eyes, wondering who Andrea's friend had been. She'd abused dozens of people, seeing them as merely hired help at her disposal. Apprehension grew into a dark knot in her chest.

"I'd like to think I'm different now," Candice said softly. "Looking back, I know I was awful. If you see your friend, will you tell her I'm sorry? Whatever I did to her, and I'm sure I made her life miserable, please tell her I'm sorry. I wish I didn't have to remember. I wish I could forget those terrible days, but they always pop up." Just like Jeremy said they would.

Andrea took in Candice's earnest words. "How could it

have been so awful? You were a star. Everybody knew you. My brother even had a poster of you hanging in his room." She pointed to Edwardo. "And you were engaged to such a gorgeous guy. Great acting roles, parties, money—it doesn't sound terrible to me."

"You're right, Andrea. None of those things were terrible. The terrible thing was who I became because of them. I hate how I used people. I hate how I acted. When I look back on that time, it feels like I'm looking at somebody else's life. But it's my own. If you stay in this business, Andrea, just be really careful."

"Can't it be that way with any business though? Why would acting change a person so much? I would think inheriting a million dollars or joining the Navy or going to college might have that same effect. It's how you choose to react to those circumstances."

Candice thought about Andrea's words. Perhaps she was right. It wasn't the acting itself that was at fault. Candice couldn't blame her circumstances for how she behaved. She alone was responsible for how she reacted to those circumstances. She never had to fall in love with fame or use her beauty to get attention. She never had to hurt people because they were in her way. She never had to be such a fool. She chose to be a fool. The revelation didn't make her feel any better. Before she could comment, a crewman zipped up the hill on a snowmobile toward Candice.

"They're ready for you, Miss Drakeforth. It's time for the chairlift scene."

"What chairlift scene?" Candice asked. She had yet to see a script or the contract that Edwardo had promised. But all the other arrangements had been finalized in such a whirlwind of activity that she'd let the matter slide. She thought about contacting her former agent but then decided against it. The man was not to be trusted, and she didn't want to be involved in a business arrangement with him again. Besides, after being away from the business for so long, she didn't know anyone she could trust.

The crewman didn't take time to answer. Instead he grabbed Candice's skis and told her to get on the back of the snowmobile. He drove her down the slope to one of the resort's smaller lifts. Each bench was just a two-seater, and the lift was two-thirds shorter than the express lifts.

Edwardo rushed over to the snowmobile and helped Candice to her feet. Candice didn't want him to touch her, but she also didn't want to make a scene. So she accepted Edwardo's assistance, much to his obvious delight. He went so far as to put his arm around her waist, but Candice quickly stepped from his grasp. Before she could create too much distance between them, Edwardo caught her hand and jerked her back against him.

"Listen up, Sweetheart. If it weren't for me, you wouldn't have this job. So try to act like you care about me." He pinched her chin between his thumb and forefinger and placed a firm kiss on her lips. "Now, let's get to work. Time is money."

Anger boiled in Candice, but she didn't say anything. Several pairs of eyes were turned her way, watching the little sideshow Edwardo presented. Already she burned with humiliation over the scene, but she didn't want to make it worse by lashing out at Edwardo. Stiffly she walked with him to where the director waited.

"Cut the lovebird act, Estanza," the director said as they crunched through the snow to where he waited. "Now I want the two of you up on the chairlift for the last scene we're shooting today. It's starting to snow again, and I want to get the scene shot before it gets too dangerous."

Candice mulled over the director's words as she followed Edwardo to the chairlift ramp. She mimicked Edwardo's moves by putting on her skis. Before she could shuffle onto the ramp, Andrea Crown ran up to her.

"Give me your gloves, Candi. You'll want to have a better grip when he pushes you out of the chair."

"What?" Numbly she allowed Andrea to pull the gloves from her hands and tape a small microphone inside her coat collar. This entire situation seemed unusual to her. She hadn't seen a script so she didn't know what was expected of her until they gave her instructions. She was doing dangerous things that were normally left to stunt people. And so far she hadn't said one word on film.

"Explain to me what's going on with this scene, Edwardo," Candice demanded through clenched teeth.

Edwardo leaned close until his head was nearly touching hers. "First, we shuffle onto the ramp and get on the lift. The lift will be running much slower than normal. When the chair is about ten to fifteen feet off the ground, they will stop the lift. One of the stunt guys will climb from his chair, across the cable, to our chair. He will then try to push you from the chair. You resist of course, but he is stronger and larger. I, too, will try to fight him off. He succeeds in his efforts. Remember this part: Grab my left wrist with your left hand and my right pant's leg with your other hand. You won't be too far off the ground. It will only look really high on film."

"This is ridiculous, Edwardo! I never agreed to be my own stunt person. Why am I doing these things, and why haven't I seen a script yet? This doesn't make sense to me—"

Edwardo put up his hand to silence Candice. "Cool it, Candi. There's no time for it right now. We need to shoot this scene."

As the director yelled "Action," Candice and Edwardo shuffled onto the chairlift ramp. Steaming with anger, she smoothed her features into an expressionless mask. She noticed that David was operating the chairlift. He gave her a wide grin, but she broke eye contact, afraid otherwise he might say something not written in the script and they'd have to start the scene over. Very slowly, the chair circled around behind them. Candice lowered herself into the seat, moving in slow motion. The chair swung into the air and carried them about ten yards. A cameraman on the chair in front of them filmed every movement. The lift stopped with a sudden lurch, leaving the chair bouncing in the air. For his sake, Candice was glad that David had followed his part to a T.

Candice looked uncertainly at Edwardo as he glanced over his shoulder. "It looks like we have trouble," he said in a low, thickly accented voice that Candice knew was his "theater voice."

"What should we do?" she asked with real fear in her voice. She wasn't afraid of the stuntman, she was afraid of falling out of the chair no matter how close they were to the ground.

Edwardo didn't answer as he watched the stuntman stand on his chair and reach for the cable that held all the chairs. As he moved forward on the cable, hand over hand, the other chairs bobbled up and down like a bunch of Christmas lights on a string. The man stared menacingly at Candice, and she actually felt that he wanted to do her harm. She swallowed hard, anticipating his next moves with dread.

The man was now hanging behind their chair. He grabbed the suspension bar and stood on the back of the seat. Candice pressed herself against Edwardo to widen the space between her and the villain. The stuntman laughed menacingly as he reached for Candice's coat. He gave her what looked like a shove but was in actuality a gentle nudge.

"No!" Candice screamed. She pushed his hand away, but he wouldn't relent. Edwardo reached around her to try to knock the guy off the chair, but he wasn't successful. Edwardo deliberately grabbed Candice's wrist tight in his grasp and made eye contact with the stuntman. In one very smooth move, Candice was pushed off the chair and found herself dangling in the air. She screamed, hoping it didn't sound contrived on film. It certainly was real to her.

Praying that Edwardo wouldn't drop her, Candice gripped his pant leg in her other hand. She didn't want to fall, even though she was about fifteen feet off the ground. If she landed with her skis still on, she would probably break a leg or injure her back. She wasn't trained for this type of maneuver.

"Hang on!" Edwardo grimaced as though he were struggling to hold her. She hoped he was just acting. As he held her suspended in the air, he battled the villain with his other hand. With great effort, he pushed the man from the chair. Candice gasped. The stunt man flew through the air and landed softly in a thick pile of powdery snow.

"Cut! That was great!" the director called, not a moment too soon in Candice's judgment.

"Now get me out of this," Candice ordered Edwardo. She knew his grip was getting tired.

"It looks like I finally have you where I want you," Edwardo grinned down at her. "I know you wouldn't want me to drop you."

"Edwardo! Pull me up!"

"On one condition, my little kiss. Go out to dinner with me tonight."

"I can't. Pull me up!"

"Promise!"

"Some other time. Edwardo, my hand is slipping!"

With little effort, Edwardo pulled Candice up, and she scrambled back onto the chair. Never had she been so glad to be sitting on the chairlift! Once she was settled, David started the lift again. Great wheels pulled the cable overhead, and the gentle whir of the motor sounded like a lullaby to Candice. She never again wanted to dangle from a chairlift.

As Candice glided off the chairlift ramp and onto the slope, Edwardo called to her. "Stop, Candi! I want to say something."

Candice stopped in her tracks at the serious tone of Edwardo's voice. He slowly and unsteadily came to a halt next to her. His face was grim as he stared down at her.

"What is it?"

"I just wanted to tell you that I'm still in love with you. I know things weren't always perfect, but I want to make it up to you. I want us back together, and I'll do whatever it takes to make it right."

As far as Candice was concerned, his penitence had come years too late. She felt nothing. All she wanted was to get away from him and go home. It had been a long day.

"Aren't you going to say something?" he asked a bit testily.

"There's really nothing for me to say. You made the choice long ago to be finished with me, and I've learned to live with it. I think we should leave things as they are."

"Didn't you hear what I just said? I said I'm sorry and I want us to start over."

"You never said you're sorry, Edwardo. Actually, I've never heard those words come from your lips. Can we just go now? I'm tired, and I want to go home." Before Edwardo could say anything more, she shoved off down the hill. Counting on the fact that he wasn't a good skier, she pointed her skis straight down the hill and zipped away from him. She didn't feel a bit sorry for leaving him stranded on the hill. He would find his own way down.

As Candice neared the base of the hill, she saw the crews scrambling to load the gear. She came to a stop near Andrea Crown. The young woman flipped her hair in the same way Candice once had.

"Oh, Candi! That was just great! I was riveted when you were hanging from the chairlift. Were you scared? I was scared for you. You are such a good actress."

"I wasn't really acting. The guy pushed me from the chair, and I screamed. Then I hung on for dear life until it was over."

As she packed up the gear, Andrea asked, "Are you going to the party tonight? Edwardo invited me. I was so surprised. I know you and I sort of look alike, but I honestly thought Edwardo Estanza would never notice me if I was in the same vicinity as you. And now I'm going out with him tonight. Can you imagine?"

"When did he ask you?"

"While you were shooting the scenes in the trees. He came up to me and offered me a thermos of hot cocoa. He is such a thoughtful man."

Edwardo had invited Andrea to a party while he was trying to get her, Candice, back in his life. She wasn't surprised that he was up to his old tricks. He probably seemed as sincere to Andrea as he had to Candice. She was glad she hadn't agreed to anything he'd asked. She only hoped Andrea wouldn't fall for his tricks and get hurt as she had. Andrea was young and pretty with her long blond hair and stunning green eyes. She had a slender, childlike face and a pretty figure. Candice knew why Edwardo was attracted to her. He had been attracted to Candice, and admitted he still was, as he had been attracted to dozens of other women. Women were playthings to him.

"Andrea, though I barely know you, I think you are a kind and hardworking woman. I also think you're very smart. Don't lose your head over Edwardo. This is coming from one woman who lost her head and was hurt badly. Don't let it happen to you." Candice hoped her sincere plea would reach Andrea and that the young woman would heed the warning.

"Are you telling me this because you're upset he asked me to the party and not you?"

Candice didn't rise to the taunt. "Please, Andrea, just be careful with him. He'll take you out. Then he'll give you small gifts of flowers and jewelry. He'll ask you to fly away with him to exotic places. But don't turn your back on him. He'll be lobbying for the attention of every pretty woman in the room when you aren't looking. And no, I'm not jealous. I'm tired and very ready to get home to my special friend."

Andrea stopped packing and studied Candice's face. "I believe you're serious, aren't you? At first I didn't think I could trust you, but now I think you're really not interested in Edwardo. I'll take your advice. And I'll let you know how it went when I see you tomorrow."

"See you then," Candice responded, but her thoughts were already on Jeremy and the quiet evening she hoped to have with him.

❧

"How did your day go?" Jeremy asked as he handed Candice a warm mug of cider. He circled the couch and sat on the opposite end, then took her slipper-covered feet and pulled them onto his lap.

Candice dropped her head against a cushion. "It was exhausting! Not only was it physically tiring, it was mentally draining. And it was hazardous to my health," she added, remembering the stunt on the chairlift.

Jeremy chuckled. "How was it hazardous? You make it sound like they had you jumping off the chairlift and falling over cliffs. Was it all bad?"

"Actually, they did push me off a chairlift. It was a scary experience that I wasn't expecting," Candice answered. Her eyelids were feeling heavy, and she closed them with a sigh.

"What?"

Candice snapped her eyes open as Jeremy dropped her feet to the floor. "What do you mean they pushed you off a chairlift? Was it an accident?"

Candice shook her head. "No, it was part of the script, I guess. For some reason they've chosen me to do all my stunt work. It's nothing I agreed to. They set up the scenes, then I find out what I'm supposed to do just minutes prior to the take. I have yet to see a script or a contract. And I haven't had one speaking part. Just skiing. It seems strange to me, but I've never worked with this director before. No one has said anything about Bryan Wright. I hope I haven't fallen for a big hoax, but I wouldn't put it past Edwardo. Acting isn't nearly as much fun as I remember."

"Are you sure you want to do this movie? If you haven't signed a contract, then you aren't obligated to continue. It would tear me up if you got hurt," he finished softly.

"I'll be okay, Jeremy. I won't do anything that will endanger me. I learned my lesson today. Anyway, tell me about the condos. How are they coming?"

Jeremy launched into a lengthy dialogue about building codes and plumbing problems. Candice felt her eyes growing heavy, though she really was interested in Jeremy's project.

Candice slowly slipped into a dreamlike state where everything was warm and comfortable and there wasn't any stress. She sighed contentedly, stretching on the couch. She felt

Jeremy pull a blanket over her but didn't comment. Instead she snuggled deeper into the blanket. He rose to leave, placing a soft kiss on her forehead.

"Jeremy?" Candice murmured from her sleep.

"Mm-hmm?" He leaned over her to hear the soft words.

"I love you," she whispered.

Jeremy studied Candice's peaceful face for several moments before moving to leave. "I'll see you tomorrow," he whispered. Quietly he grabbed his coat and went to the door. Making sure it was locked behind him, he left the apartment.

nine

"Can I ask you a favor?" Candice asked when Jeremy picked up the phone. She knew her request might be refused. After all, Jeremy was very busy with his condos.

"What do you need?" Jeremy asked, his voice softening.

"Would you be willing to come to the set with me today? I don't have a lot of confidence at this time, and your presence would be a boost for me. Plus, if there's something strange going on, you might be able to pick up on it."

"You've got it," Jeremy agreed. "Just give me enough time to give directions to my foreman."

"We're filming at the summit lodge. I might even have a speaking part."

"Yeah, we'll see, huh?" Jeremy added caustically. They were both remembering that she hadn't seen a script. "Will it work if I get there by ten?" he asked.

"Perfect!"

Candice rang off, feeling more confident about the film than she had earlier. She quickly prepared for the day by pulling her hair back into a simple ponytail and dressing in her ski pants and a white T-shirt. She didn't bother with makeup because that would be taken care of on the set.

She drove to the resort, but before riding up the chairlift to the lodge, Candice stopped at the ski patrol office. She wanted to check in with her boss just to make sure everything was going well in her absence. She didn't want to forsake her steady job for the one-time acting part. As she walked into the cluttered room, she expected to find it empty. Instead she was surprised to see not only her boss and a few ski patrol members but also the resort's manager, Mr. Calloway.

"Well, if it isn't the movie star!" Craig announced to the room as Candice stepped inside. Several people turned to study her, including Mr. Calloway. Candice felt her cheeks flood with color.

"Stuff it, Craig," she muttered as Mr. Calloway moved toward her.

"Miss Drakeforth, I'm glad you stopped in. There are some things I want to discuss with you."

All activity in the room stopped as everyone strained to overhear the conversation. Thankfully Mr. Calloway was conscientious of privacy and led Candice into Chief's office and closed the door behind them. Chief stood just inside the doorway. He winked at her to show his support but remained silent. The serious undercurrents concerned Candice, and she studied the men to find what this was about. Their expressions were stiff and unreadable.

Mr. Calloway wordlessly pointed to a chair, and Candice sat. She watched him walk around Chief's messy desk, covered with papers. He picked up a glass paperweight with a palm tree floating in it. He seemed unconcerned as he stared at the paperweight. Candice's apprehension grew as she waited.

"I want to know what's going on up there," Mr. Calloway said calmly. He waited for Candice's answer, making her squirm under his direct gaze.

"I don't understand, Sir."

Calloway set the paperweight down on the desk. "I know there's something going on up there. The director won't answer any of my questions or return any of my calls. We had an agreement. They were to pay a fee for using the resort's resources. Something of a rent or deposit. I have yet to see a dime, and it was to be paid before filming began. The other part of the agreement was that you were to have a part in the film. Have they fulfilled that part of the arrangement?"

Candice paused, uncertain how to respond. Had they actually fulfilled that part of the bargain? There was no script, no contract, no speaking parts. "I guess they haven't really fulfilled that part of the agreement either," she said with conviction. Edwardo had made many promises to her, and none had come to pass. "After filming several scenes, I'm still uncertain of my role in this film. I'm not even sure it's really a Bryan Wright film."

Calloway slapped the desk. "I knew it! I knew I couldn't trust that actor or his director. Something didn't seem right to me when they agreed to my terms. I have it all in writing too, of course."

"Sir, what actor?"

"Edward something or other. Now what I want you to do is go up there today and keep your ears open. Find out why they aren't keeping their part of the agreement. Remember, you're still on this resort's payroll. Do you think you can do that?"

"Of course. I'll find out what's happening, and I'll let you know," Candice promised. She rose from her seat and shook the manager's hand. Then she turned to Chief.

"You watch yourself up there," he warned. "I don't want you getting hurt." He affectionately patted her shoulder.

"I'll be careful. And I'll check in soon," she added.

The entire situation seemed odd, and Candice was glad she wasn't the only one to notice. It would help to have Jeremy there. While she worked, he could snoop around.

Candice arrived at the top of the mountain just minutes before Jeremy. She was glad to have him there right away so that she wouldn't have to face Edwardo or the director alone. She suddenly felt self-conscious, as though she held a secret, but she feared it was written all over her face. After Edwardo took one look at her, he would know she was up to something. She didn't like the subversive tactics she might have to take to get information, but it was necessary. If Edwardo or the director was using the resort, it wasn't right, and the truth had to be told. In a way it was like acting another part. She hoped no one would be able to see through her.

"Jeremy! I need to talk to you before we go into the lodge," Candice called as soon as she saw him.

Jeremy placed a warm kiss on her cheek and took her cool fingers in his.

"Can't we go inside first? It's pretty cold up on this mountain."

Candice shook her head. "I need to talk to you out here where I know we won't be overheard. My boss has some concerns, and I need your help to get to the root of things." She quickly filled him in on the details. "So you see, we need to find out why they aren't paying and what's really going on."

As Candice led the way into the lodge, warm air surrounded them and warmed their faces. Andrea rushed toward them, breathless and frantic.

"Candi! Where have you been? The director has been screaming for you, and nobody knew where you were. We have a stunt to shoot, but you need to be ready first."

Candice turned helplessly toward Jeremy as Andrea grabbed her arm and started dragging her toward the ladies' room. He waved her forward.

"Don't worry about me. I'll keep myself busy," he said with a wink.

Candice allowed Andrea to help her change clothes. Then she did Candice's hair and makeup faster than Candice thought possible. Candice tried several times to extract information from Andrea, but the younger woman wasn't talking. She either had hairpins in her mouth and couldn't answer, or she would suddenly rush out of the room saying she needed a different type of hair spray.

"Something is going on here. And I will find out," Candice muttered. Finally, she was ready for filming.

"Don't forget your goggles," Andrea called as Candice left the room.

Edwardo was waiting for her just outside the ladies' room. His scowl was wide and his eyes stormy. "Who's the guy, Candi? I thought we were going to try to work things out."

Candice looked across the lodge and saw Jeremy talking with one of the cameramen. *Good,* she thought, *he's already on the job.*

"You met him, Edwardo. Remember? His name is Jeremy Braunfeld. He and I are good friends."

"How good of friends? As good as you and I were?" Edwardo asked through clenched teeth.

Candice brushed past him, unwilling to answer his question. How dare he be jealous when he was dating Andrea on the side? He probably had several girls waiting in line as well.

"I'll show you that I'm the man for you, Candi. You'll see. Once you remember how good we were together, you won't give that other guy another thought," Edwardo called after her.

Candice cringed at the words. She didn't want to remember what they were like together. She wanted to forget those days. Every time she saw Edwardo, he reminded her of the terrible things she'd done in the pursuit of fame and fortune. Perhaps working on this new movie was a bad idea. It made her face things daily that she wanted buried deep in her past.

Forcing all unpleasant thoughts from her mind, Candice

hurried to the set where the next scene was to be filmed. The director's face was red and turning redder as he shouted to one of the cameramen. Candice felt sorry for the cameraman. She knew what it was like to be on the receiving end of a director's fury, and it wasn't pleasant. Perhaps if she intervened, she could take some of the heat off the young man, who looked like he wanted to sink through the floor.

"Are we filming inside the lodge?" she interrupted, moving near the director. The director shot her an annoyed looked, but she ignored it. The cameraman was obviously relieved with the interruption. "If we're inside, don't you think I'm a little overdressed? Goggles, scarf, coat, ski pants. I might melt into a puddle. And while I'm talking to you, can I get a copy of the script? If you want me learning lines, I'm going to need one."

The director suddenly looked uncomfortable, all thoughts of the cameraman forgotten. "A script, you say?" He paused, looking around the room. Candice wondered if he was looking for someone to rescue him. "I. . .ah. . .why are you asking me?" he blustered. "You actors need to take care of things like this yourself! What are you bothering me for?" He raised his hands and stormed away, leaving Candice to puzzle over his strange behavior.

"No script?" someone asked softly against her ear. Candice smiled at Jeremy's nearness.

"Nope, it's very strange. He got upset when I asked him about it. So I wonder what I'm doing today." She turned to look up at Jeremy.

"I can tell you that. The cameraman who was getting an earful before you rescued him filled me in on the day's events. And I'll just bet he was reprimanded for talking to me. Makes me even more curious about all this."

"So what part do I play today?" Candice prompted.

"You won't be inside, and you won't have any speaking parts again. They have you being pushed off the two-story deck of the lodge into a snowbank. Then you grab a pair of skis, they miraculously fit your boots, and you take off down the mountain with two goons in pursuit."

"No speaking parts again. And I'll bet they want me to wear goggles the entire time," Candice mused.

"Did they ever tell you how big a role you are playing in this movie?" Jeremy asked.

"Not specifically. I get the feeling that the part is shrinking. I wonder if my name will even show up in the credits by the time we're done filming."

Jeremy turned his attention to Andrea Crown, who was just coming out of the ladies' room. She was dressed in ski clothes similar to Candice's. Candice was struck again by how young and pretty her assistant was.

"I think I might know what's going on here," Jeremy said suddenly.

Candice drew her attention back to Jeremy. He was still watching Andrea move around the lodge. An irrational twinge of jealousy pricked Candice, but she quickly dispelled it. Jeremy would never two-time her like Edwardo had.

"Look at that girl over there. Isn't she your assistant?"

Candice turned again to watch Andrea. She smiled and flirted with all the men just like Candice used to do. Suddenly a switch flipped in Candice's mind and everything made sense. Andrea wore the same clothes, had the same hairstyle. Candice wore goggles and did all the skiing. Andrea was the star, and Candice was the stunt double!

Just as Jeremy was about to divulge his thoughts, Edwardo crowded between them, pushing Jeremy to the side.

"Edwardo!" Candice glared at him, but he ignored her ire.

"Come on, Candi. It's show time. Send this guy home so we can get started." His arm snaked around Candice's waist, and he tried to draw her to him but Candice resisted. Instead of drawing attention, Edwardo received the rejection quietly. "Just hurry up. We're waiting on you," he ground out before storming away for his final costume check.

"I have to go," Candice said reluctantly. Jeremy's look made her knees turn to jelly, and nothing else mattered. Would he ever admit his feelings to her, or would he always let them shine through his eyes as they were now? When he didn't respond, Candice slowly backed away from him.

"Wait!" Jeremy grabbed her hand and pulled her back. He placed a quick, firm kiss on Candice's lips in front of the entire crew.

"What was that for?" Candice asked, feeling a bit dazed.

"For success. Go do your thing; I'll keep my eyes open around here. Just be careful."

❧

"Why would I stand here?" Candice asked a short while later as she looked over the rail from her perch atop a table. The drop to the snow below looked very long and dangerous. And the bank didn't look as soft as they'd promised it would be.

"When Edwardo tries to block the stunt double's attack, you will take a step onto the table. As Edwardo is unable to block the attacker from reaching you, you will step fearfully backward. Your legs will press against the rail, causing you to look down. The attacker will try to reach you, and instead of being caught by him, you will jump over the rail and into the snowbank below. Your skis will be waiting nearby, and without another thought, you will pop on the skis and take off down the slope."

Candice again looked at the steep drop to the snowbank.

Could she make the jump without hurting herself? She wasn't trained to take those kinds of falls. She shook her head and stepped down from the table. "I'm not doing it," she said quietly but firmly. Nobody seemed to hear her. It didn't matter to her that everyone ignored her as they readied for the shoot. She pulled off her goggles and gloves and searched the crowd for Jeremy. She was ready to leave. This movie was ridiculous, and she wanted no part of it any longer. It confirmed to her that her acting career was in the past, and it was time for her to move forward. Regardless, if she had some unfinished issues, this was not the way to have them resolved.

As she was wending her way through the people, the director shouted her name.

"Candi! Get over here! We're wasting time. Get over by the table so we can get started. Places everyone!"

Candice stared in amazement as everyone scrambled into place. Everyone came to attention but Candice. Slowly, she backed out of the commotion until she was on the outskirts of all the activity. She knew that when the director found her out of place he would erupt, and she didn't want to be anywhere near the source.

"Going someplace?"

Candice turned to find Jeremy moving through the people toward her. Candice nodded. "I'm done here, and the sooner I leave, the better."

"Good. I wasn't going to let you risk your pretty little neck by jumping off the deck. They're fools to expect such a thing."

"I would have been an even bigger fool had I gone along with their plan."

Jeremy put his arm around Candice and began leading her through the doors into the lodge.

"Where is Candi Drakeforth?"

Candice cringed at the sound of her name being thundered out of the director's mouth. She knew by the sound that he was angry, and nothing short of groveling would appease him. At one time she might have been willing to grovel in order to save her career. She felt Jeremy's gentle pressure at her shoulder. It gave her courage. She lifted a determined chin and turned to face the director.

"Get in place, Candi!" the director yelled. All eyes turned to stare at Candice. She felt her courage waver but knew she couldn't give in. It was her life they wanted to risk.

"I'm not doing it," she answered softly yet clearly. A hush fell over the crowd. She felt Edwardo's steely gaze upon her, but she wouldn't look in his direction. She no longer cared what he thought of her.

"Don't be ridiculous. We don't have time to play these games."

"It's not a game. I'm not doing it," she answered firmly. She accepted Jeremy's warm fingers wrapped around hers as he led her out of the crowd and through the quiet lodge. Everyone stared as though frozen in place.

"You can't walk out on this shoot! You're in breach of contract!" the director yelled. Candice could imagine his face turning bright red with agitation, but she was too far away to see him. Both she and Jeremy grinned at each other over the director's ridiculous words.

"What contract?" she snickered. Jeremy's deep chuckle joined hers.

Candice and Jeremy parted ways with a promise to meet that evening. Jeremy went back to the condos to see how the workers were progressing. Candice went to report to her boss. She stopped uncertainly in the doorway of Mr. Calloway's spacious office. Walking off the movie set hadn't been what

Mr. Calloway had planned for her to do. He wanted her to collect information, not quit the job. She hoped he wouldn't be angry because of her brash actions. She also hoped she hadn't put her ski patrol job in jeopardy.

"Mr. Calloway?" she called from the doorway, tapping on the open door.

Mr. Calloway swung around in his chair, greeting Candice with a warm smile. "How's my favorite movie star?"

Candice threw him a worried look. "Unemployed. I walked off the job today. I hope you aren't angry. I know you wanted me to collect information and watch for motives, but they wanted me to do something dangerous, and in good conscience, I couldn't do it."

Frowning, Mr. Calloway studied Candice. "What did they want you to do?"

"Jump off the deck of the summit lodge. They must think my abilities are far greater than they are."

"And you didn't want to jump?"

Candice shook her head, wondering if she'd made the right choice. "No, I didn't want to jump."

Mr. Calloway slapped his desk. "I agree! I think it's time to get them off my mountain. We'll take care of this right now." He grabbed his jacket and quickly crossed the room to the door. "Let's go."

Candice could imagine what it would look like if she showed up with the resort manager ready to send the movie crew packing. It was something like a child facing the bully with her dad. "I don't think I should be a part of this, Sir. I'd rather they didn't link me with your decision. I hope you understand."

Mr. Calloway nodded his agreement and left to deal with his unwanted guests. Candice hoped that he wouldn't be forced to call security or law enforcement, but she knew her presence wouldn't improve the situation. She was ready to get home and put the day behind her. First she needed to talk to Chief about the schedule, but then she could go home and wait for Jeremy to come over.

About an hour later as Candice headed toward her Subaru in the parking lot, she realized Edwardo was waiting for her. Her heart pounded at the sight of him. She wondered when she would forget how she'd loved him years earlier. His gaze was unreadable as he watched her approach the car. He was always good at hiding his feelings.

"You made us lose the movie, didn't you?" he accused. His tone was calm and warm, but Candice wasn't fooled. She knew his anger was merely shielded by a veil of civility. Her eyes narrowed as she waited for him to continue.

"What I don't understand is why you went crying to your boss before talking to me. We could have worked it out. Whatever you were upset about we could have tried to fix it."

Candice rolled her eyes. "Give me a break, Edwardo! You never wanted to work with me. There was no script, no contract, no acting part for me. You thought you could fool me. 'Stupid Candi, I've worked with her before. She'll do anything.' I know exactly what you were thinking. You wanted me to do all the stunt parts while my so-called assistant, Andrea Crown, did the actual acting. Can't Andrea ski? Well, maybe she shouldn't be in a ski movie."

The more she spoke, the angrier she became with Edwardo. She was tired of being used by him. He had used her years ago, and he was using her again. It wasn't any different. As much as she had once loved him, she now despised him even more.

Edwardo moved toward Candice, his eyes glinting with

shards of steel. He put his hands on her shoulders. His fingers gripped the tender flesh, making Candice wince. "You have no idea what you're talking about. There is more at stake here than you know. You think you can brush me off and throw away this project, but it doesn't work that way, Candi Kiss. You and I go way back, and you know how I work. I'm an all or nothing kind of guy. I want it all this time, Candi girl, and I won't let you stand in my way."

A different look entered his eyes, one that was calculating yet less hostile. Candice felt his pinching grip on her shoulders ease. "You just need to be reminded how good we were together. Your boyfriend isn't around, and your eyes are sending me a message—"

"No, they are not, Edwardo. I don't want anything from—"

"Oh, yes, Candi, your eyes are telling me you want me back in your life. You miss the excitement we had together. Your words argue with your heart. And I will believe your eyes and ignore your words."

Before Candice could retort, Edwardo pulled her against him and forcefully kissed her. She pushed against him, but he wouldn't release her. His lips bruised her tender mouth, making her cry out. Finally, he released her.

"Stop it, Edwardo! Can't you understand how I feel? I don't want anything to do with you. I thought maybe I still loved you, but I don't. Sometimes I feel like I hate you."

Edwardo threw back his head and laughed. "That was the best acting I've ever seen you do, Candi Kiss. I almost believed you. I'll go now, but don't worry. I'll be back tomorrow. We'll straighten things out then."

Candice watched Edwardo go, wishing he had never come to her mountain. Slowly she climbed into her car and drove to her apartment. Her thoughts whirled, constantly replaying the scene. Edwardo infuriated her and stirred up so many emotions that she thought had perished long ago. She wished the emotions were dead because then she wouldn't have to deal with them. She immediately regretted the harsh words she'd thrown at Edwardo, though at the time she'd meant each one. She didn't want to hate anyone, not even Edwardo. But he didn't care about her callousness; he'd hardly reacted to her words.

But Candice cared. The entire scene left her disgusted. Weary and upset, she was glad to finally be home. Slowly, she trudged through the fresh snow to her doorway.

"Please, Lord, help me deal with Edwardo. I don't know what to do about him and it's making me sick."

&

Two hours after her encounter with Edwardo, Candice was waiting for Jeremy to show up as they'd planned. She continued to look out her window, hoping to see his approaching form, but each time she was disappointed.

"Something has happened, I just know it," she muttered. "He wouldn't stand me up like this." A nagging worry hung at the back of her mind. When the shrill ring of the phone sounded, she was startled out of her seat. She rushed to answer it, hoping it was news of Jeremy.

"Candice?" Jeremy's familiar voice sounded strained.

"What is it, Jeremy? Has something happened?"

"Candice, someone vandalized the construction site. Windows are broken, and someone sprayed red paint across the back of the condo." His words grew quieter with his anger. "And I know who did it. It was a threat."

"What? Who would do such a thing?"

"Edwardo Estanza is behind this. At first I thought it might be a rowdy group of kids pulling a prank, but the message in red paint was too direct for a prank. It said, 'The show must go on. . .or else!' "

Candice gripped the phone tighter. "And you think Edwardo wrote it?" she asked, dread filling the pit of her stomach.

"Who else would have done it? All I know is that my building project is going to be on hold until I can get this mess straightened out. My insurance will cover the damage, but the work will stall while a claim is filed. I can't believe this happened when the project was going so smoothly."

"Jeremy? This is my fault, isn't it? If it hadn't been for me quitting the movie, Edwardo wouldn't have come after you. Jeremy, I'm so sorry."

"Hey, listen, Sweetheart, this isn't your fault. But I need you to understand that I'm going to be busy trying to get things back on track. Don't think I'm ignoring you, okay?"

"Jeremy, I'd really like to go over and see the damage. I have to see what Edwardo did."

The line was silent as Jeremy hesitated. "All right. But let me come get you. I really don't think you should be going out alone at night. Who knows what that guy might do? I don't want you to get hurt. Give me a few minutes here, then I'll come get you."

Jeremy's face was grim when he arrived a few minutes later to pick up Candice. She could understand his frustration. Edwardo had done something childish because he was angry, and it wasn't fair that Jeremy had to pay for such foolishness.

"Are you sure you want to see it?"

Candice nodded. "I have to know. I have to see it for myself."

The drive to the construction site was quiet. Jeremy was lost in his own thoughts while Candice replayed her earlier conversation with Edwardo. He seemed so angry, yet so determined. She wondered if he linked his failed relationship with the failed movie. Perhaps he thought if he got Jeremy out of the picture, Candice would come to him willingly and the movie would be placed back on track. Well, she had news for him. She was done with the movie, and she was done with him.

Jeremy pulled his truck up to the condo and left the engine running so he could shine the headlights at the building. Ugly red paint was sprayed along the wall. "The Show Must Go On—Or Else." The hostile message made Candice shiver. Why would Edwardo stoop this low? Was he so desperate?

"All but two windows on this unit need replacing. Thankfully we haven't got the carpet in yet, or it would be a real mess with all the snow."

"Are you sure your insurance will cover this?" Candice asked quietly. The vandalism made her sick and furious at the same time.

"I've already contacted them. A claim has to be filed, but it should go smoothly. Thankfully I have good coverage. They sent out an agent to assess the damage. His assessment along with the police report should make the claim go through faster."

"The police have been out here? Do they know it was Edwardo?"

"They said it looked like common vandalism, that it wasn't a personal attack. The officer said a construction site across the valley was complaining of the same problems." Jeremy shook his head with frustration. "I just can't believe a couple of kids would do something like this for fun. It's too coincidental. The movie was shut down today, then I get a message on the wall saying the show must go on. The cop, unfortunately, didn't want to take the time to follow it through. So it's being treated as a random act of vandalism." Jeremy paused, letting out a deep sigh. "Only you and I know differently."

Candice strode back to the pickup with Jeremy in tow. "Take me home, Jeremy. I need to talk to Edwardo about this. He can't think he'll get away with this so easily."

Jeremy caught up with Candice and gripped her arm. "No! Don't do anything, Candice. What he wants is for you to retaliate. He's trying to get you on his terms. If you confront him, he'll think he has won."

"But, Jeremy, if I don't confront him he'll think he's won. I know what he's doing. He thinks he can make you leave me. If he pushes you hard enough, you'll give up because I'm not worth the fight. I have to talk to him and ask him to leave you out of this."

Jeremy stepped closer, his eyes flashing with anger that Candice had never seen. She took a step back from him. "I'm in this, Candice. When he messes with someone I care for, he messes with me. I don't care about the vandalism. I care about you. He can't do anything to change that. So don't go talk to him. Promise me you won't."

Jeremy waited for Candice's promise. She didn't want to give it. She wanted to go over to Edwardo's hotel and give him a piece of her mind. He deserved a severe tongue lashing at the very least. Even more, he deserved to go to jail or be fined. To do nothing was too much for Jeremy to ask. "I have to do it for you, can't you see?"

Jeremy stiffened. "No, I don't see. Don't go over there, Candice. He's using me to get to you. Don't give in to these games. Promise."

Candice sighed. She still didn't see it the way Jeremy did, but she didn't want to allow Edwardo to drive any distance between her and Jeremy. "I promise, Jeremy," she whispered. "I promise I will do nothing while he tries to destroy you because of me."

Jeremy chucked Candice under the chin, trying to lighten the mood. "I'm a big boy, Candice. I can take care of myself. Edwardo doesn't scare me. He can't do anything to hurt me." He paused, staring down at Candice. "Actually he can do something to hurt me, and that's if he hurts you. Don't let him hurt you," Jeremy pleaded softly.

Candice shook her head. "I won't, Jeremy. I won't let him come near me."

ten

The next several days were a struggle for Candice. Edwardo's behavior made it difficult for her to keep her promise to Jeremy. Edwardo called repeatedly every day. As she prepared for work the phone would ring, and as she walked through the door at the end of her day, the phone would again ring. Never did Edwardo mention the damage to Jeremy's construction sight, though Candice knew he was waiting for her to bring it up. The longer he went without comment, the more Candice knew Jeremy had been right. If she confronted Edwardo about the destruction, she would be giving him ammunition. It might even cause him to do more damage.

"You realize I'm going to win," Edwardo said one evening when Candice picked up the phone. She had just gotten off work and planned on having a light supper with Jeremy at their café.

"Who is this?" Candice taunted. "You must have the wrong number. Good-bye." Without allowing Edwardo another word, she hung up the phone. She didn't have time to play his silly games. Jeremy was probably on his way over, and she still needed to change from her work clothes.

Choosing her favorite skirt and a soft sweater, Candice quickly dressed. The skirt was long and silky with small powder blue flowers on a navy background. The lightweight sweater was the same light blue as the flowers and felt like a warm fuzzy blanket. She hoped Jeremy would like what she'd selected. She then ran to the bathroom, freshened her makeup, and put her hair up in a clip at the back of her neck. Just as she slipped on her shoes, the doorbell rang.

"Do you want me to get it?" Lindsey called from the kitchen. "I know you've had a problem with your fiancé lately."

"He's not my fiancé!" Candice answered from the bathroom. "And let me get it. It's Jeremy!" With a last glance in the mirror, she hurried down the hall and yanked open the front door.

"Hey, Gorgeous," Jeremy greeted as Candice opened the door. "Are you ready to go?"

Candice nodded, blushing under his approval. She grabbed her coat and allowed Jeremy to help her into it. He then took her hand and tucked it in the crook of his arm. "Let's go. I want a quiet table in the corner with you."

At the café, Candice couldn't take her eyes off Jeremy. The more she knew of him, the more he appealed to her. He was right in the middle of telling her about his childhood when he stopped abruptly.

"What, Candice? Why do you keep looking at me like that?"

Candice sat straighter. "How am I looking at you?"

A lazy grin spread across Jeremy's face. "Like I'm your hero. If you don't quit, I might develop quite an ego. Besides, you're the movie star. I should be hanging all over you!" he teased.

Candice shook her head. "Not anymore! I'm just a skier, and there's nothing special about that. No more movies for me."

Jeremy reached across the table and laced his fingers with Candice's. "I think there's plenty special about you," he murmured.

Before Candice could respond, the waitress approached their table. "A gentleman asked me to give this to you." She slid a wide envelope across the table to Jeremy.

"Who?" Both Jeremy and Candice looked around the small café but didn't see anyone they knew.

"He's over there." The waitress pointed toward the far wall, then frowned. "Well, he was there just a moment ago. I'll be back, folks, to see if you need anything else."

Jeremy reached for the envelope and tore it open. "Wonder what this is about," he muttered. Slowly he pulled out a large photograph. "Oh!"

Candice suddenly felt sick with dread because of Jeremy's dark expression as he looked at the picture. "What is it?" She snatched the photo out of his hands. When she recognized the picture she closed her eyes, hoping to shut out the image. It was a photo of her in a skimpy bikini, walking arm in arm with Edwardo. The shot had been taken while they were filming on the beaches of Mexico.

"I'm sorry, Jeremy. You have to realize it was taken before I was following Christ," she tried to explain. "I'm so embarrassed." She folded the picture in half and set it on the table between them. Both stared at it as though it were a poisonous snake.

Jeremy took the picture without looking at it again and stuffed it into the envelope. "It's just another one of his ploys, Candice. Please don't make more of this than it deserves. He's hoping that one of us will overreact."

Candice clenched and unclenched her hands in her lap as her thoughts raged. Edwardo had no right! He had no right to destroy the best relationship she'd ever had. She needed Jeremy's friendship and his trust, and Edwardo was trying to steal that away. "Jeremy, I'm so angry right now. I don't think I've ever been this angry. I hate what he's trying to do. He's trying to make you leave me." Her eyes suddenly filled with tears as she thought of the possibility. "I don't want to lose you."

"Oh, Candice, please don't cry. I admit that I don't like the picture, but I'm not angry about it. He's just trying to find my limitations. What he doesn't realize is that I'm a very patient man and I've found someone worth waiting for. Remember when I said that I'm a big boy? I can deal with this one too." He gently rubbed his fingers over Candice's knuckles. "Now smile, or I'm going to take you ice skating again, my little penguin."

Candice laughed and hiccupped at the same time. "I'm definitely not going ice skating!"

❧

The next few days were quiet. Edwardo stopped calling, and Candice wondered what he was up to. She knew he wouldn't give up that easily, and she imagined he was disappointed the picture hadn't done any damage. She was waiting for the next shoe to drop and hoped it wouldn't be the one that found Jeremy's limitations. She didn't want to discuss Edwardo with Jeremy anymore. She knew her ex-fiancé made him uncomfortable, not to mention all the terrible things Edwardo kept doing to Jeremy. It was definitely best to keep Jeremy out of it. Candice needed to talk with someone about her troubles, and she knew just the person: her sister.

Candice picked up the phone and quickly punched Claire's number. It rang several times, and Candice was afraid her sister wasn't there. Finally, on the fourth ring Claire picked up.

"Hello?" came the sleepy voice.

"Did I wake you? Claire, I really need to talk to you." Candice could hear Claire stifle a yawn.

"I was just napping. I get so tired in the afternoons. What's on your mind?"

Where should she begin? "This might be a long conversation

so I hope you have time. Here goes. It was Edwardo who called you, just like you thought. He needed to find me because he wanted to make a movie at my resort." Candice continued to fill in her sister about the movie and the way Edwardo treated her. "Claire, I've finally met someone special." She knew her sister would get excited with those words.

A sound like a shout and a laugh came over the line. "Who is he? What does he look like? He's a Christian, right?"

Candice smiled at her sister's enthusiasm. "Slow down, Claire. We don't want you to start into early labor. His name is Jeremy Braunfeld. And yes, he's a Christian. Actually he's the most wonderful man I've ever met. And you know what else, Claire? I think I love him, and Edwardo is trying to chase him away." She related the incidents of vandalism and the terrible photograph.

"I've never been so angry, Claire. Isn't it enough that he tried to ruin my life one time? He definitely ruined my career. Now he's trying to ruin my chance with a good and sincere man." Her voice shook with emotion as she thought about Edwardo. He was manipulative and selfish. And she couldn't let him hurt her anymore.

"You have to forgive him," Claire said gently. "You have to forgive him for all he's done to you."

"I can't," Candice answered flatly.

"You have to. Ask God to help you." The line crackled, but Claire's words came through clearly.

"I can't, Claire. I can't pray about him, and I can't even talk to him. He doesn't realize he needs to be forgiven so why should I bother?"

"Candice, you know why you need to forgive him, for your own peace. Also, Jesus commands us to forgive because of what He has forgiven us for."

Candice sighed deeply. "I know the Scripture, and I know you're right. But I just can't bring myself to do it."

"Until you deal with your past, you won't be able to move on. It will be like a stone tied around your neck, dragging you to the bottom of the sea. Deal with it, Candi, and let it go."

"You sound just like Jeremy."

"He sounds like a good guy. Just think about it, Candi. You know I only want the best for you."

"I know. And I also know it's time to end this conversation. My phone bill goes up each month."

ىۋ

Candice was glad to be back to work at the resort. Working with the movie crew had convinced her that she was through with the film industry. Edwardo had said she needed to redeem herself in the eyes of the entertainment world, but she disagreed. Her career as an actress was over because of her choice, not because of that one humiliating audition.

Even though the film crew was supposed to be packed up and on its way back to California, Candice didn't have any work to do with the ski patrol. When it looked like the movie was going to take several weeks to shoot, Mr. Calloway had Chief mark Candice off the schedule. All of her shifts for the next few weeks were assigned to someone else. Chief gave her two options: end her work season early or fill in as needed in different departments.

Candice wasn't ready to call it a season so she opted to help out where she could. Lindsey was thrilled to have her help for a day with ski school. Candice hoped she would enjoy it more than Lindsey did.

The first day in ski school, Candice had the beginner class. All the children in her class were six years old or younger, and none of them had ever been on skis. It was Candice's job to outfit seven little kids with ski equipment. The room was chaotic. The kids wanted to cooperate but didn't know what they were supposed to do. And each one possessed that sweet childish curiosity that drove them all over the room, checking out everything. If Candice could get one to sit still, three would try to disappear. Thankfully another employee assisted her with fitting boots, helmets, and goggles. Candice tried to stuff little hands into mittens as the assistant adjusted ski bindings to fit all the boots. After almost an hour, all the children were bundled into winter gear and had their skis ready to go. Candice wondered what it would be like on the mountain.

Lindsey pulled a cart loaded with all the children's skis and helped Candice shepherd the children from the building to the bunny hill. The kids walked like robots in their stiff ski boots, making Candice laugh. It was difficult for them to stay upright, but they managed. Lindsey didn't think it was so funny. It was just another day on the job for her. They walked a few yards to the bunny hill where the smallest children were taught the basics of skiing.

"Do you want help getting them into their skis?" Lindsey asked, shivering. She had forgotten her coat and glanced longingly at the warm building.

"No, Lindsey," Candice answered, taking pity on her roommate. "I can manage it from here. Just come get us when it's time for lunch."

"Oh, no, you'll come inside long before lunch. Your class will have an hour out here. Then you'll come back in for snacks and cocoa while the next group goes out. After snacks, the kids color little pictures of bears skiing. Next is a movie and play time, then you'll have lunch."

"Wow, I had no idea there was such a rigorous schedule. Just keep me on track because I'll forget what we're supposed to do." Candice reached out to redirect one of her charges. The little guy was trying to escape, but he couldn't move too fast in the boots.

"See you in an hour!" Lindsey called over her shoulder. Candice could hear her roommate laughing. Candice would show her. Working with kids was what you made of it. It was either fun or a chore. Candice intended to have fun.

Candice guided her little troop into the fenced-off area and marched them up the gentle incline to the top of the bunny hill. Candice thought the sidewalk to her apartment was steeper than the ski hill so the children shouldn't have too many problems. Next she instructed them to put on their skis. It took several minutes of patient coaxing before the last child was ready to go down the mountain. Candice remained in regular snow boots so she could better instruct the children.

"Now before we go down the mountain, I want to give you a few instructions."

Seven pairs of eyes turned to Candice expectantly. "We're going to make our skis look like a piece of pizza. Watch this." She showed the children how to point their toes inward so that the ski tips made a triangle or "pizza." Each of the kids imitated her action. They each had their feet turned inward and arms stretched out to their sides. Candice chuckled at the sight. They looked like seven little penguins. Jeremy would be so proud!

"Great! Now I'm going to walk partway down the hill, and when I call to you, I want you to come to me one by one. Does everyone understand?"

Seven little heads nodded. "Good. Now I want Cody to come down first since he's on the end."

Candice walked to a midpoint and stopped, then waved for the first little boy to come toward her. He skied a few feet, then fell over. "That's fine, Sweetheart! You did a great job. Can you push yourself up?"

After a half hour of one-on-seven training, Candice's little group was beginning to show some improvement. Candice, however, was becoming weary. Once a child made it to the bottom of the bunny hill, Candice had to pull him back up to the top. When they fell and couldn't get up, she had to lift them. It was tiring work, and she could see why Lindsey came home exhausted day after day.

Lindsey finally appeared after what seemed like an eternity, but only an hour had passed. "Who needs a snack?" she called to the children. All the little kids cheered. "Well, let's get out of those skis and go back inside!"

Several activities followed, making the day go quickly. Candice helped color, led kids to the bathroom, wiped noses, located missing gloves, and cuddled the inconsolable. By the time the last child was picked up, she was exhausted.

"I don't know how you do this every day," Candice muttered to Lindsey on the way home. "I love kids, but they wore me out." She dropped her head against the headrest and closed her eyes. "You don't suppose having your own kids will be this hard, do you?"

"I think it will be different. Maybe not easier, though," Lindsey answered thoughtfully.

After a moment, Candice said, "You'll be sorry to hear that I'm leading a snowshoe tour tomorrow. I could use a break from all those kids."

"You were there for only a day!"

Candice sighed deeply. "I know, and already I need a vacation."

≈

Shortly after Candice got home, Jeremy appeared on her

doorstep with a pizza in his hands. "I thought you might need this. Pepperoni, mushroom, and green pepper," he said when Candice swung the door open. "How did it go with all the kids?"

"It wasn't bad. I really do like little kids. They just wore me out." She took the pizza from Jeremy and led him into the kitchen. The aroma of green peppers was enticing and made her stomach growl. "I can't believe you remembered what I like on my pizza," she commented.

Jeremy just smiled. He grabbed a couple bottles of cola from the refrigerator and tossed one to Candice.

"I never knew they had so much energy. I had to keep them from climbing the walls. But then when they got tired, they crashed. They were all lying on the floor, watching a movie when their parents showed up. A couple even fell asleep. I wanted to curl up next to them."

"So does that mean you want kids of your own?"

Candice didn't miss the serious note in Jeremy's tone. She took out a slice of pizza and handed it to Jeremy. "I would love to have my own children."

"Me too."

After an awkward moment of silence, Candice changed the subject. "I'm leading a snowshoe tour tomorrow. Would you like to join me? I'll give you a fabulous discount and world-class trivia about the mountains."

Jeremy shook his head regretfully. "I'd love to, but I can't. There are a few things with the building project that need my attention. And that's part of the reason I'm here tonight. I wanted to tell you that I'm going to have to spend a lot more time with the condos if I'm going to stay on schedule. A few things have put me behind."

Candice thought about the vandalism. It was her fault

Jeremy had to work extra hours on his project. If Edwardo hadn't pulled that foolish prank, Jeremy would still be on schedule. Add that to all the time he spent with her, like going cross country skiing, and it was no wonder he was behind.

"Jeremy, do whatever you need to do. I'll understand if you can't spend much time with me. Those condos are the whole reason you're here, and I can't be the reason you get off track. Maybe we can spend a little time here and there. And when the ski season is over and the condos are finished, we can decide where we go from here. Until then, we'll both be working."

"I certainly can't argue with that logic." Jeremy leaned close to Candice and kissed her cheek. "I'm glad you understand. If I could, I would spend every minute with you. But the condos would suffer, and my uncle would fire me—"

"And you can't lose another job because of me!" Candice interrupted.

"If I can't see you, you'll know it's because of the condos and nothing else. Right?" Jeremy asked, making sure she understood.

"Of course. I trust that if anything is ever wrong, you'll tell me and won't leave me guessing."

Jeremy nodded. "And you do the same." When Candice nodded, Jeremy continued. "I have to go and make a few calls tonight before it gets too late. Enjoy the snowshoeing tomorrow."

Candice rose and followed him to the door. "If you call me tomorrow night, I'll tell you all about it."

Jeremy briefly kissed her. "You can count on it."

❧

Leading the snowshoe tour was much easier, though not as entertaining as the ski school. Together with a group of ten tourists, Candice rode up the chairlift to the top of the mountain. She then showed them how to strap on the awkward-looking snowshoes and how to use them.

"Slip your boot into the straps. There's a metal pick directly under the ball of your foot. You'll use this part of the snowshoe to help you on inclines."

Once everyone was ready, Candice led the group along the snowshoe path, deep into the trees. The trail was narrow, moving down the mountain in a wide, zigzag pattern. She loved the peacefulness of snowshoeing. The only sounds were the slap-slap sound of the snowshoes as they scuffled along the trail. The tall pines towered overhead, allowing the warm sunlight to break through the snow-covered branches. Off the trail the snow was deep but not too deep for chipmunks and rabbits. The tourists saw a few of the furry little animals and had to stop to take pictures. As they approached mild inclines in the trail Candice encouraged everyone to lean forward so that the snowshoe pick would dig into the snow. And as they went down, she showed them how to lean back slightly on their heels to engage the heel pick.

The tour was less than two miles long, but with the high altitude, Candice allowed many breaks for the tourists. On each of the frequent breaks she shared her knowledge of the resort and the mountains in general.

"Take a look at the aspen trees." The guests all turned to look at the many white tree trunks with bare branches. "Aspens are the largest organism in these mountains. All of the trees are connected by a large root system underground. Though they appear to be individual, each tree is a part of the system. Now if you'll turn to look at the valley below, you'll see the resort. In the months of January and February this resort hosts many competitions for professional skiers. It also holds several different tours for those who enjoy activities other than skiing. You can tour the mountain on snowmobile or take a moonlight sleigh ride. In the summer months some of the runs are open to mountain biking, and of course there's great shopping in town. There are also excellent hiking trails all around the area."

She answered a few questions about the resort before leading the guests back to the trail. "We'll finish the tour without any more breaks. So unless you have any last questions, let's get back on the trail."

The rest of the tour was quiet and gave Candice time to think. She wished Jeremy had been able to join the tour. She knew he had to work, but he probably would have enjoyed the break. It would have made the experience more enjoyable for her too. While she loved to snowshoe, she was glad to be tour guide for only one day. The routine would quickly grow monotonous. As the tour ended at the lodge, each of the guests thanked her, and a few gave her a small tip. Candice, too, was thankful. She was glad to have another day away from ski patrol done.

As soon as she got home, she found an envelope slipped under her door. She quickly tore it open and pulled out the card. It had a picture of a penguin on skates. Candice laughed at the cartoon. Inside the card was a note:

I'm sorry I can't see you, and now I can't even talk to you. I have meetings tonight with subcontractors and won't be able to call. Please forgive me and know that you are always in my thoughts.

All my affection,
Jeremy

With a sigh of disappointment, Candice closed the card. She had hoped to talk to Jeremy. The thought of hearing his voice had helped her through the day. Now she wouldn't even get that much. And why had he signed the card, "All my affection"? Couldn't he have just put "Love, Jeremy"? Candice knew she loved him. Didn't he feel the same? She wished she could just call him and ask him. She wanted to know if he had his heart involved or if she was just a nice distraction during his project in the mountains. To keep her evening from dragging slowly because of so many questions, Candice went to bed early. Finally, she was to be back with ski patrol the next day.

eleven

When Candice walked into the ski patrol office, she knew something wasn't right. Edwardo was talking with Craig. Just the sight of him made her stomach turn over with dread and sudden anger. She felt the muscles tense in her back and her teeth clench.

She hadn't seen Edwardo for several days. He hadn't called her, either, so it was a surprise to find him in the office. She'd hoped he had given up on her and left the mountains. His film crew was supposedly headed for California, and Candice had hoped Edwardo would be with them. Unfortunately he was still around and still very confident. She watched him as he shared an animated conversation with Craig. She wasn't sure which man had the bigger ego. What made her curious, though, was why Edwardo was talking to Craig. She didn't realize they knew each other. It didn't matter to her how they met. What did matter was that trouble was brewing. She just knew it.

Cautiously she slipped through the room and sneaked over to Chief's office. She didn't want to endure Craig's sarcasm, and she didn't want anything to do with Edwardo.

She found her dear supervisor behind his desk, growling at the computer screen. He didn't even look up when Candice stepped in front of his desk.

"Glad you're here, Candice. Help me with this schedule, will you? I don't know why they want me to use a computer. Paper has always worked just fine in the past."

"Speaking of schedules, do you think you can put me back on patrol full time? I'm missing the slopes," Candice asked as she circled the desk. Chief rolled back in his chair to allow Candice room to work. With a few corrections, she had the schedule ready for him.

Chief shook his head, amazed. "You did that so fast. You make movies, you ski professionally, and you're a computer whiz. Is there anything you don't do?"

Thoughts of Jeremy's troubles and Edwardo's intrusion entered her mind. "If I could handle men as well as I fix ski schedules, my life would be perfect."

"Sorry, I can't help you there. And yes, I've got you back on the schedule. But to complicate matters, you're spending the day with Craig. I know you've had problems in the past, but I can't discriminate. You're both on snowmobiles."

Candice groaned inwardly but didn't let her displeasure show. Snowmobiles meant more idle time listening to Craig brag about his mastery of the fairer sex. Ugh! Yet Chief was right. She couldn't discriminate against Craig. She just had to make the best of a difficult situation.

Exiting the office with Chief behind her, Candice strode over to Craig and Edwardo. She ignored Edwardo's appreciative gaze as she addressed Craig. "It looks like we're partners again today. Chief wants us at the base with backup snowmobiles. I'll wait outside for you." Candice zipped up her red coat, waiting for Craig's smart comment. When it didn't come, she looked at him in surprise.

Craig waved at Edwardo. "I'll see you later, Buddy." Edwardo nodded in assent, then winked at Candice.

"I'll see you both later," he called.

Wordlessly Candice walked with Craig to where the Arctic Cat snowmobiles were parked. She chose the newer model,

Thundercat 1000. She loved the power and quick response of the snowmobile. It even had hand warmers in the handle grips. It was longer than most snowmobiles by about a foot. With long cleats on the track, it was designed to do better in thick powder. The front skis skimmed over the powder, and the whole package made for a fun ride.

When Craig didn't argue over her choice of snowmobile, Candice became even more wary of him. Whenever they were paired together, he always chose the Thundercat before Candice had a chance to speak. She wondered what he was up to. And she hoped his plans had nothing to do with Edwardo.

"Well, Movie Queen. It looks like it's just you and me today. So while we're sitting here waiting for a call to come down the mountain, let's talk," Craig said as he straddled the older model snowmobile.

Candice eyed him warily. "What do you want to talk about?" *And since when are you interested in me?* she added silently.

Craig shrugged. "Tell me about Edwardo Estanza. I hear things are pretty hot between you."

Candice's eyes flashed with sudden irritation. "It's about as hot as Antarctica. There's nothing between Edwardo and me. Who told you this?"

"Edwardo. He said that once the movie is done, you're going back to California with him. He also said there is a part for me in this movie he's filming. All I have to do is teach him some snowmobile moves. Then I'll do some of the more challenging moves in the movie as his stunt double."

"You have got to be kidding!" Candice stared hard at Craig. "He still thinks he can make the movie here. And to top it off, he's tricked you in the same way he fooled me. Don't fall for this, Craig. He's using you just like he used me. Besides, Mr.

Calloway will never go for it."

Craig stood, his eyes blazing as he glared at Candice. "Now wait just a minute! Just because you couldn't get along with the crew doesn't mean you have to ruin this for me. He said you were jealous of Andrea Crown and couldn't stand having her in the lead role."

"He said that? He said I was jealous?" Candice asked, incredulous. This was too much. Edwardo had a lot of nerve to say such things about her. Of course, he didn't mention how he'd manipulated her to get his own way.

Craig nodded. "Yeah, he said those things. And you know what, Movie Queen? I don't care what's going on with you and him. Just don't mess with my chances to get in a movie, and we'll get along fine. This movie will open up many opportunities for me."

Candice rolled her eyes but didn't comment. Of course Edwardo was able to convince Craig to work with him. All he had to do was appeal to the man's ego. If it would make Craig look good, Craig would do anything. Candice just hoped she wouldn't get stuck in the middle and take any more blame.

The day was quiet as far as ski emergencies went. On one call that Candice took, a teenager had wrenched his knee while snowboarding. Another lady broke a finger when she fell. Candice was relieved there weren't any serious accidents requiring air evacuation by helicopter. Around four o'clock, Craig got a call on his radio. Candice tried to piece together the brief conversation.

"I'll pick you up at the upper lodge. Right, the one where the film crew was working. Be there in about five to seven minutes. Yep. I'll tell her." Craig turned to Candice. "Put on your gear. We're going to the top," he instructed.

Candice obeyed by pulling her goggles down over her eyes

and zipping her coat up to her chin. "What was that about? It wasn't a normal call, was it?" she asked, suspicious.

Craig shook his head. "Nope. We've got a little training on the back of number two mountain." He pull-started his snowmobile, and the engine roared to life.

"I don't remember Chief saying anything about a training." It was normal to have refresher training in outdoor emergencies, avalanche, and mountain survival. Yet she didn't remember any scheduled trainings for that afternoon. "What is this about, Craig?" she demanded, but Craig continued to gun the engine so he couldn't hear Candice over the noise. Slowly he drove away from Candice, dodging all the skiers loitering at the base of the mountain.

Uncertain of what to do, Candice decided to follow Craig. She pull-started her snowmobile, and the Thundercat vibrated with restrained power. Candice was glad she'd chosen the more powerful machine since Craig had something up his sleeve. She knew this "exercise" wasn't right, but she had to stick with Craig since they were partners for the day. If she allowed him to go alone, someone might get hurt, and she wouldn't be available for backup.

"Lord, whatever this is about, please give me wisdom in how I handle myself," she muttered through cold lips. Craig was several yards ahead, zipping straight up the mountain. He hung close to the trees along the side of the ski run to avoid most of the skiers. Candice followed him at a slower pace, keeping her eyes open for any skier who might need assistance.

In a few short minutes they reached the top of the mountain and the summit lodge where Candice was supposed to have jumped from the balcony. She was relieved to find the camera crew absent and only a bunch of skiers sitting at the tables, sipping coffee and eating sandwiches. Everything appeared normal. The only thing she didn't see was the ski patrol training team.

Craig pulled the snowmobile to a stop near the rear of the lodge, shut off the engine, and climbed off the machine. Candice followed his example. She wanted to ask him some more questions, but Craig seemed in no mood to discuss his plans. Instead he walked around to the front of the lodge.

Candice came to an abrupt stop when she found Edwardo waiting for them on the stairs. "What is going on here?" she demanded.

Craig turned to face her. "We're going to train Edwardo on snowmobiles today. Since it's a slow day up here, there should be no problems."

Candice threw him an irritated look. "Are we training him for ski patrol, Craig? Give me a break! Let him hire someone. Don't use company time. Did Chief okay this?"

Craig's boots crunched in the snow as he approached Candice. He stopped when he stood mere inches away, towering over Candice. "Listen to me. I have the seniority here, you don't. And unless you want me to file a report against you, you'll do as I say. Our job is to oblige the customers and see that they are safe. If we don't go along with Edwardo Estanza, he's going to do this on his own and put himself in jeopardy, possibly others. He also specifically asked that you come along. If it weren't for his wishes, I'd tell you to take a hike. He wants you here, so you're staying." He poked his finger into her shoulder. "Got it?"

Glaring up at Craig, Candice nodded. "Got it. But there better not be any funny business, or I'm going to write that report. You got it?"

Craig nodded too, his eyes steely as he stared down at her. "Glad we see eye to eye," he said, his expression grim.

Abruptly he turned to meet Edwardo, a wide smile on his face. Candice was surprised at what a versatile actor Craig could be.

"You're driving Candice's snowmobile. She'll ride with you. Just follow my lead," Craig instructed.

"No way, Craig! He can't handle the Thundercat. It's lighter than yours and overturns more easily. You know that!"

Craig ignored Candice's outburst. "You'll be fine. The Thundercat is a zippy machine, and you'll love it. It responds real well, just like a Jet Ski on water."

Candice was about to argue more, but Craig threw her a warning glare so she clamped her mouth shut. How did she ever get into these situations? If Claire were with her, she would just shake her head in wonder. Candice always found trouble without bothering to look for it.

Studying Edwardo, Candice had to admit that he did look good. He wore black ski pants and a black ski coat that had a wide yellow stripe around the middle. She noticed with great relief that he had a helmet. At least he wouldn't crack his fool head open. The helmet was also black with a yellow stripe, perfectly matching his coat. She assumed he would wear the ensemble in the movie. *I wonder if he'll get to finish the movie,* Candice thought. She watched him strap on the helmet, then pull on his gloves. He nodded to Craig.

"Great! Let's go," Craig announced. He climbed on his snowmobile and started the engine. Candice watched Edwardo approach her snowmobile. He swung his leg over the seat, then turned to her expectantly.

The last thing Candice wanted to do was come in close contact with her ex-fiancé. She didn't want to touch him, let alone press against him as they rode the snowmobile. Edwardo must have contrived this situation. It worked perfectly to his advantage. The best thing she could do was pretend indifference. If he didn't know she was troubled by the contact, it would take away some of his satisfaction.

With a businesslike air, Candice strode over to the snowmobile and straddled the wide seat behind Edwardo. "You need to start the snowmobile," she instructed, pointing to the pull-start on the right side.

Edwardo jerked on the starter, and the machine roared to life. Candice wished she had her own helmet. She didn't usually wear one when she aided injured skiers. In daily operations she never drove quickly enough to need one. Gently, Edwardo gave it some gas, and the snowmobile moved forward across the snow. Candice gripped Edwardo around the middle, disliking the contact. Yet she had no alternative but to hang on to him. If he gave the powerful machine any more gas, she would fly off the back end and land in the snow.

Craig pointed to the narrow snowmobile trail that led into the trees. Edwardo nodded and followed Craig's lead. He drove cautiously, slowing on the narrow turns and letting out the gas gently. The trail was smooth, and the powder wasn't too thick so the going was easy for Edwardo.

"I think I'm getting the hang of this," Edwardo shouted after several minutes on the path.

Candice didn't respond. Instead she concentrated on keeping as much space open between her and Edwardo's back as possible. Though she still hugged him around the middle, she refused to press against him. The effort was beginning to make her back and neck ache, but she couldn't give in. She wouldn't give him the satisfaction.

Finally, they came out of the trees and into a wide clearing. The sun reflecting off the snow was bright and warm, and Candice breathed a sigh of relief when Craig and Edwardo pulled the snowmobiles to a stop. Candice quickly jumped off the back of the snowmobile to put space between her and Edwardo.

"So how many miles per gallon does this baby get?" Edwardo asked Craig.

Craig shrugged, "About ten or so. Depends on how much hot dogging you do. You can make it about one hundred miles of even driving."

Candice put her hands on her hips. "I think he has the hang of it, Craig. We should probably get back down to the base and check in with Chief," she suggested.

"Don't worry so much," Craig snarled. "I have a couple of the other guys covering for us this afternoon. We have plenty of time."

Edwardo nodded. "Yeah, I've got a handle on the basic stuff. Now I'm ready for some of the stunts."

"What do you mean 'stunts'? We don't do any stunts on this mountain," Candice interjected.

Craig laughed. "Listen to 'little miss prim and proper.' Of course we can do some stunt training. There's no one else up here. It'll be perfectly safe." He pointed to Edwardo. "Just don't forget who taught you these moves!"

Edwardo laughed. "You got it! You and I can do the stunts in this film just like Candi did all the female ski stunts."

"And just where are you going to be filming the rest of your movie, Edwardo? From what I understand you didn't fulfill your end of the agreement with this resort. Do you have a new place to do the filming?" She tried not to sound catty, but she couldn't keep the triumph from her voice. For once in all the time she had known Edwardo, she finally had the upper hand.

Edwardo winked at Craig. "I'm getting things worked out.

Don't worry your pretty little head about the movie. You'll still have a part."

"A part! I don't want a part in your silly movie. If you think you can film on this moun—"

"Let's go," Craig interrupted. "We're wasting daylight. There are some perfect hills we can use as jumps at the bottom of this slope. Just follow my lead."

"Jumps? No way! I'm not going to be a part of this! You're not supposed to do those things with company vehicles, Craig, and you know it. Count me out!"

"Do you plan on walking back?" Craig challenged.

"I'll just call someone to come get me," Candice countered. She pulled out her radio with a triumphant smile. The smile quickly died when she realized the batteries in her radio were low.

"Looks like you're coming along for the ride, Movie Queen. Better jump on before you're left behind." Craig's laugh echoed across the quiet mountain. It grated on Candice's nerves and rubbed her ego. Stiffly she walked over to where Edwardo waited on the snowmobile. She didn't bother to look at him as she climbed on the seat behind him. Edwardo smiled invitingly, but she ignored him.

"Listen, Candi Kiss. Try to make the best of this. I know I shouldn't have asked you along, but I wanted you with me."

"I'm trying not to hate you, Edwardo, so save your words," Candice ground out. She couldn't even look at him without being angry.

"You are just confusing your emotions. You don't hate me. You know you still love me. Face it. And I still want to work things out. I couldn't think of any other way to get you alone with me since you won't even talk to me. Perhaps this was a stupid gesture. But I thought if we spent the day together, some of that ice around your heart would melt a little toward me."

"Don't count on it," Candice muttered. Nothing that Edwardo could do or say would make her feel charitable toward him. It was wrong for him to use Craig, and it was wrong for her and Craig to be in this situation. And as far as anything that came out of Edwardo's mouth, Candice believed none of it. Finally, she was learning.

Edwardo shrugged. "My patience toward you won't last forever. You'd better stop playing hard-to-get before I stop chasing you."

Before Candice could retort, Edwardo revved up the engine so no words could be heard. He swung a tight, fast turn, spraying snow. Candice gripped Edwardo tightly around his waist to keep from being thrown from the snowmobile. She could sense that Edwardo was laughing at her reaction, and it infuriated her.

Craig led Edwardo through a series of sharp turns. Snow sprayed in all directions, blinding Candice, and she had to grip Edwardo tighter than she liked in order to stay seated. The ride was rough, and she felt insecure as the passenger of a novice driver. Had she been the driver, it wouldn't have been a problem. The Thundercat was a powerful machine, but she could handle it. She was experienced in traversing rough terrain with it. Edwardo, however, was only experienced at driving a car.

"Here we go, Candi Kiss!" Edwardo whooped. "We're going straight for those jumps!"

Candice could barely hear him over the engine, but she knew what he meant. "Lord, please help us," she groaned. If Edwardo didn't hit the small jump squarely, he would tip the vehicle. Or if he made the jump soundly but didn't hold the steering, he could lose control. Candice closed her eyes.

She could hear the whine of the engine as Craig hit the jump, then landed soundly. She knew she and Edwardo would hit the jump in seconds.

Edwardo punched the gas, and the snowmobile shot forward. They raced toward the small hill. An outcropping of exposed boulders and a clump of pines stood to the far right of the hill. Candice prayed that Edwardo wouldn't lose control and smash into the rocks. Edwardo hit the hill at an angle, causing the snowmobile to fly a few feet off the ground and tip violently to the right toward the outcropping of rock. Both Edwardo and Candice were thrown from the vehicle.

Candice felt her body fly through the air as though she was suspended. Her head hit something hard. She didn't know what she hit, but it wasn't soft snow. Before she could open her eyes, everything went fuzzy.

twelve

When Candice awoke, she was greeted by an incredible headache unlike any she'd ever experienced before. It felt like the entire right side of her face was swollen and throbbing. She wanted to open her eyes, but it took too much effort. With an agitated groan, she tried to roll over but couldn't. Her ribs burned, and her right arm felt heavy and immobile. Gingerly she reached over with her left hand and touched her right arm. She found her arm encased in a cast from her upper arm down her to her wrist. No wonder it felt so heavy.

"Hey, Honey, are you waking up?" came a soft feminine voice.

"Claire." Candice forced out the word through dry lips that felt like hardened clay. The sound came out as a low croak. She groaned again with frustration.

"Do you want a drink?" her sister asked.

Candice nodded, immediately regretting the action. Sharp needles of pain shot through her head with the motion. She felt a cup press against her lips and tried to take a sip.

"Here, use the straw. It'll be easier," Claire instructed.

The water cleared a path down Candice's throat, refreshing her parched mouth. She tried to open her eyes but was blinded by the bright light and had to immediately close them again.

"The doctor says you have a concussion and that you're lucky to be alive. But we know better than that, and I told him luck had nothing to do with it. You also broke your arm in two places when you fell and cracked a rib. That was some crash. What were you doing with Edwardo? I was scared to death when they called me last night. Mom and Dad are even on their way here from Montana."

"Last night? What is today?" Candice croaked.

"It's Thursday. Yesterday was Wednesday when you had the accident. You regained consciousness a few times in the night. You don't remember? They gave you medication for the pain. Your boss, Chief, came this morning. He's angry with the situation but not at you, of course. I think he said the other guy was fired. I can see why you once said he reminds you of Dad. He seems to care for you."

Jeremy's image floated through Candice's mind. "Has Jeremy been here?" she asked, afraid to hear the answer. Perhaps he didn't even know that anything was wrong. He had a lot going on with the construction. If no one informed him, he would have no idea she was injured.

Before Claire could answer, her husband, Rick, came into the room. "Hey, Candi. You doing okay? Don't you think you should take it easy with the extreme sports?"

Candice smiled at his teasing tone. He was the one who jumped from airplanes and climbed mountains. Snowmobiles were tame for this man. "I'm glad you're here, Rick. You are treating my sister well, aren't you?" She tried to look at him without opening her eyes too wide.

"Yep. I won't let her have too much ice cream, and I even go to the store at three in the morning when she craves cheese-covered pretzels. Then when she gets heartburn I sit up with her all night long."

Candice grinned at the pride she heard in Rick's voice. "You'll be a good dad, Rick. I just hope you're willing to change messy diapers."

"No problem! I've got a book telling me all about it. Now we just have to figure out how we're going to get Aunt Candi to our house so she can recuperate. We still have a bed in the guest room, but there's a crib in there too."

Candice tried to sit up, but the pain shooting through her side and head forced her to lie back against the pillow. She took a moment to answer as she fought sudden dizziness and nausea. "I won't be staying at your house, but thanks anyway. Maybe I'll go stay with Mom and Dad. I could always go snowmobiling on their ranch," she added with a small smile.

She closed her eyes, feeling overly drowsy. *Must be the medication,* she thought. The soft answering chuckles of Claire and Rick faded into the background as Candice drifted to sleep. Jeremy's image wavered in her mind as the last thing she thought of before she slipped into slumber.

Waking a few hours later, Candice didn't feel any more rested than she had earlier. Added to her grogginess, her side was throbbing, and it felt like someone was beating a bass drum in her head. She reached for the water glass on her little tray, ignoring the rip of fire that went through her side when she moved.

"Feeling better?"

Startled, Candice turned to find Edwardo sitting in the chair next to her bed. His feet were propped up on the edge of her bed, and his arms rested behind his head. He looked quite comfortable, and it irritated Candice.

"What do you want?" she asked testily. She wasn't in the mood to play his games anymore. Why couldn't he just go back to California and leave her alone? Hadn't he done enough damage in her life?

"You look pretty banged up," he commented. "All I got was a scratch on my arm." He pulled up his sleeve to show her a long, deep scratch down his forearm. Candice turned away with disgust.

"I've been thinking about us, and I've also been talking to your sister. She's really nice," he added.

"Leave my sister out of this, Edwardo. She has nothing—"

Edwardo held up his hand to stop Candice's outburst. "Listen to me. This is something I should have said a long time ago, and I think you really need to hear it. Are you going to let me speak?"

His serious tone silenced Candice's anger. Nodding tightly, she said, "Go on."

"When you said I've always used you, that wasn't entirely correct. Remember how we were together?"

Candice held up her hand. "I don't want to think about those days."

"Listen! When we first met and were engaged, I truly thought I cared for you. You had spunk and real talent, albeit raw talent. You had passion, and you were young and beautiful. I just couldn't resist you. You were like a kitten with needle-sharp claws. I couldn't keep away from you. Then I met Maureen."

"The woman you married, right?" Candice faintly remembered the unknown actress who had arrested Edwardo's attention.

"Almost married. She actually left me at the altar, but that's not something I tell everyone. She had money, and money is something every struggling actor wants. She dangled it in front of me like a carrot before a mule. Such a mule I was. She used me to undermine your career. She's the one who wanted you to try out for that part. Remember the audition where you forgot your lines?"

Candice rolled her eyes. "Don't remind me. It was the most

humiliating day of my life."

"You wouldn't have gotten the part anyway. Maureen had the scripts switched on you. You were learning lines for a different part. She set you up to fail."

"It seems I would have failed anyhow, so she didn't need to go to so much trouble," Candice added dryly.

"When you left town, I felt really bad," Edwardo continued, "but I was so ensnared by Maureen that there was little I could do to mend things between you and me. I honestly thought she was the one for me. Then she let me in on how she made all her money. She's a thief."

"Oh, come on, Edwardo! Is this another one of your stories? It's a good one. I almost fell for it."

"Candi, do you know where I've been for the last three years?" He waited for Candice to answer. Slowly, she shook her head.

"I've been in jail."

Candice's eyes widened with surprise. "You were in jail? No way!" she exclaimed in disbelief. The grim look on Edwardo's face convinced her he was telling the truth. "I had no idea. Why didn't you ever try to contact me? All that time passed, and I thought you were married and living the 'happily ever after' story."

"I wanted you to think that. I didn't want you to find out that I was in jail because of Maureen. It was so humiliating. She set me up to do one of her jobs. She steals rare paintings, jewels—anything rare and valuable she can get her hands on. She worms her way into people's lives. Finds out their secrets. Then she hires someone to pull the job. As the stuff is being shipped out and sold, she's holding the victim's hand and giving him condolences. She and I were on shaky terms before the job. When I got caught, she and I were finished.

She wouldn't even help me get a good lawyer."

"Was it bad, like in the movies?"

"Worse. It was the most humiliating time in my life, and I deserved every minute of it. The good thing is that Maureen was finally caught too. It took the authorities awhile to track her down, but she's still serving her time."

"So why did you come here to make a movie? I can't believe you convinced me Bryan Wright wanted to produce a film for you. Bryan Wright doesn't know my name. What is your real reason for finding me after all this time?"

"You're right. I lied about Bryan Wright to get you to do the film. I knew it was the only way I could get you to work with me. You're too smart to do a no-name film. I wanted to get back into movies, but I couldn't find anyone to back me. Then I came across Lester. He was willing to direct and produce the film. I got a fairly decent script from a film student. And when you spread word that you're making a movie, everyone else just flocks to you. That's how I found Andrea Crown—"

"My assistant, right?" Candice couldn't keep the accusation from her tone.

"Well, not exactly. She was supposed to play the lead in the movie. I promised her. We were going to film it in California, but when I found you here, all the pieces fit in place. We needed a ski resort and someone who could really ski. You provided both. I was looking for you for personal reasons, but your circumstances fit all my needs. You could ski well. You were in good with your resort. And best of all, you looked just like Andrea with a pair of ski goggles on."

"Why didn't you just tell me all this from the beginning? I hate that you lied to me and played me for a fool."

"I didn't think I could tell you the truth. You would have

shut the door in my face. So instead, I tried to appeal to your professional side. I thought that if I dangled a movie part in front of you, you would do whatever I wanted."

"Like the carrot in front of a mule?"

Edwardo shrugged, caught by his own words. "Touché." He paused as though searching for the right words. "Here's the part I've been needing to say for a long time." He took a deep breath, looking down at his hands. "I'm sorry. Really sorry. I'm sorry for setting you up and having you humiliated at the audition years ago. I'm sorry for making you think I didn't care for you any longer when I was so confused about my feelings. I should have talked to you instead of making you a public spectacle. I'm sorry for coming here and using you again. I'm sorry for the accident and almost killing you. I've been conniving and manipulative, and I've made a mess of everything. When I said I wanted you back in my life, I was telling the truth. But most of all I need to ask your forgiveness."

"You want me to forgive you?" Candice asked, incredulous, yet wanting to believe he was finally telling the truth.

Edwardo nodded earnestly. "I need you to forgive me."

"It isn't that easy." Candice turned away so she wouldn't have to look into his pleading eyes. "You didn't just hurt me. You hurt Jeremy too. You vandalized his construction site."

"I know, and I'm going to pay him back every cent I destroyed."

"And what about the picture of you and me? That was a low blow, Edwardo."

"All I can say is I'm sorry. I didn't like having competition, and I thought if I showed him how far you and I go back, he would get mad and leave."

Candice smiled gently at the thought of how Jeremy had handled everything. He had been right. She'd wanted to rip

Edwardo limb from limb, but Jeremy had convinced her to take a step back and let everything play itself out. He was a stronger man than Edwardo could ever hope to be. He was strong because of his character. Only God could produce that kind of character.

Candice then allowed her thoughts to travel back to that day when she'd stood on stage in front of the agents, casting directors, and the producer. Everyone had laughed at her. Edwardo had deserted her. She'd been alone and mortified. Then the anger came, followed by the pain. Thankfully her sister had been there for her to help pick up the pieces.

"You really hurt me," Candice whispered. The humiliation seemed so fresh, as though it had all happened just days before and not years. A tear slipped from the corner of her eye and trickled down her cheek. "No man ever hurt me in such a way."

Edwardo reached over and brushed away the tear. "I know. I'm sorry."

Forgive him. The silent words sounded as a gentle command to her spirit.

Candice suddenly realized this was the moment for which she had been searching for so long. She was at a crossroads. She could forgive Edwardo for all the pain he'd caused her. To take that path would be a difficult first step. Yet every step after that seemed to hold life and promise. Or she could harden her heart toward him and turn him away. He deserved to be rejected as she had been rejected. He deserved to know what it felt like to open your heart only to have it trampled. It would be easy to crush him in his vulnerability as he had with her.

Forgive him.

Candice narrowed her eyes at Edwardo. He stared back at her, his dark eyes waiting expectantly, almost anxiously for her answer. Her thoughts shifted to Another who also waited for her answer. One who was perfect, yet died on her behalf. Her choices weighed before her, the decision became simple.

Candice swallowed hard, knowing what she needed to say. "Edwardo, I do forgive you. I forgive you because Christ forgave me. How can I not offer the same grace to you?" As the words left her mouth, Candice knew she really meant them. The anger, pain, and hatred that she'd carried for three long years vanished. Suddenly she was free from the prison that had held her captive for so long. As she embraced her decision to forgive Edwardo, chains fell away from her soul. She was like a dove, free to spread her wings and fly to the heavens. She closed her eyes with a contented sigh. It was all about forgiveness. "I'm free," she whispered. "Finally."

thirteen

Jeremy stared at his watch and scowled. Daylight was fading, and the work crew still didn't have the new windows in yet. He wanted to see Candice. She probably thought he didn't want anything to do with her. The last time he'd seen her, he should have told her that he loved her. She had been so upset about that picture. Instead, he'd skirted the issue. She needed to hear how he felt, and he really did want her to know. Yet for some reason he held back.

Then the condominium project started taking all of his time. He had been so busy trying to get the construction back on track that he hadn't taken time to see Candice. Even though the project had started smoothly, it wasn't finishing that way. Workers didn't bother to show up. Wrong supplies were shipped. Invoices didn't match. It was frustrating work, but nothing he couldn't handle. His uncle trusted him to take over the business, and Jeremy had to prove he was up to the task. All he needed was time. Every morning he was up by five, and he rarely made it into bed before midnight. What work he could do, he did himself, and he was often working right alongside the workmen. His strenuous hours didn't make for a very secure relationship. He hoped Candice would understand.

"Come on, guys! What's the holdup?" he called. One of the men peeked his head out the gaping hole in the side of the condo.

"It won't fit, Boss!"

Jeremy took off his hard hat and rubbed his head. *I won't*

get mad, and I will not yell, he reminded himself with a deep breath. "What do you mean, 'It won't fit'?"

"I tell ya, it's the wrong size," the guy called.

"I'll be right up," Jeremy answered. He rushed into the condo and up the flight of stairs into the room where the workmen were trying to install the new window. Jeremy immediately located the problem and was relieved it was a small oversight and not actually the wrong-sized pane.

"You're putting in the wrong one, guys. The one you have goes downstairs." He pointed to another pane, similar in size but smaller, lying against the far wall. "Try that one. I bet it'll fit like a glove." He watched as the men traded the panes of glass, then installed the correct one. It slipped into place just as Jeremy had hoped.

"While you're finishing up here, I'm going to make a quick call. Holler if you need anything."

"Sure thing, Boss."

Jeremy went to the kitchen where he already had a phone installed in the condo. His cell phone didn't work well in the mountains so he had to install a land line in the condo. He quickly punched Candice's number, hoping she would answer. On the fourth ring, someone picked up.

"Candice?"

"No, this is Lindsey, her roommate. Is this Jeremy?"

"Yeah, this is Jeremy. Do you know when she'll be in?" he asked, trying to tamp down his disappointment.

"Jeremy, didn't you know?" Lindsey paused. "She's in the hospital."

"What? You have got to be joking!"

"No, I'm serious." As Lindsey quickly filled in Jeremy on the details of the accident, Jeremy jotted down the necessary information, then bid a hasty good-bye. He ran up the stairs to where the workmen had just finished the window.

"Guys, there has been an emergency, and I've got to go. I'll probably be gone a few days. Finish up downstairs, then lock up for me, will you?"

Barely hearing the workers' response, Jeremy ran down the stairs and out to his truck. He felt like his heart was in his throat with thoughts of his Candice lying injured in a hospital bed with no one there for her. It made him sick to think she could have died without knowing how he really felt about her.

The drive to the hospital was short, but Jeremy felt like it took hours. He parked his truck in the first available spot, then tore into the hospital. Jeremy rushed down the hospital corridor, counting off each room number as he passed it. The place seemed so quiet and sterile. He really didn't like hospitals.

"Room 223. Good," he muttered under his breath as he pushed through the door. He expected to find Candice lying in bed greeting him with a warm smile when he entered. What he did not expect was to see Edwardo Estanza bending over Candice's sleeping form and pressing a kiss to her temple. The sight filled him with rage, and he had to take a step back.

Edwardo looked up and saw Jeremy in the doorway. "Oh, it's you." His tone wasn't hostile; neither was it inviting.

Jeremy pictured Edwardo throwing bricks through the windows of his condo and spray painting the exterior. He thought of that gut-wrenching picture of Edwardo and Candice walking on the beach. He shifted his gaze to focus on Candice's broken body in the hospital bed. Hot, furious blood pumped through his veins. "What are you doing here?" he asked, his voice low but intense.

Edwardo took a measure of Jeremy before answering. "I needed to talk to her," he finally answered. "She and I have worked out a few things." He threw Jeremy a triumphant grin.

Jeremy cast an uncertain glance at Candice, but she couldn't respond. He watched Edwardo reach for Candice's hand. In her sleep, she curled her fingers around his. Jeremy swallowed hard. Had he left her alone too long? What had Edwardo said to win back her affections? If they had worked things out as Edwardo said, then there was no room for Jeremy. Whether or not Edwardo had been a liar and a manipulator in the past was irrelevant. It was safer to just back away.

"I see. Well then, I'll just come another time," Jeremy said unevenly. Without another look at Candice, he backed out of the room. Edwardo resumed his place next to the hospital bed, and Candice continued in her slumber, oblivious to the turmoil Jeremy felt.

Jeremy stormed down the hospital corridor, berating himself for being such a fool. He loved her. His heart ached because he loved her so much. And yet he'd allowed his one true love to be drawn away by that manipulator. Would it have mattered had he revealed his feelings sooner? It didn't matter now. With a groan, Jeremy sagged onto a stiff sofa placed at the end of the corridor near the elevators. He was so wrapped up in his torturous thoughts that he didn't hear the elevator open. When two people stepped out of the elevator, he ignored them.

"Rick! Be serious! I do not eat like a horse!" a woman laughed. The sound was agonizingly familiar.

Jeremy looked up, then stared in astonishment. The woman looked like Candice and sounded like Candice, yet by her condition she was obviously not Candice! The man nodded at Jeremy in a friendly way, then put his arm around the woman as they walked. Jeremy continued to stare. The woman stopped and turned to him.

"Are you Jeremy?" she asked.

Jeremy nodded stupidly, unable to turn away. The resemblance was incredible.

"My name is Claire. I take it Candi has never mentioned me."

Jeremy scrambled to his feet. "Uh, not exactly. Well, she said she had a sister, but I had no idea—"

The man laughed and slapped Jeremy on the back. "Join the club, Man! I had the same reaction. These two left my head spinning." He stuck out his hand to Jeremy. "My name's Rick Spencer. I'm Candi's brother-in-law."

Jeremy shook Rick's hand, still awestruck. It never had occurred to him that Candice was a twin.

Claire laughed at the dazed look on Jeremy's face. "Let's go talk with Candi. She'll enjoy hearing about this meeting."

The mention of Candice froze Jeremy's humor. "Uh, no. I don't think that's such a good idea. She has another visitor right now."

"Oh, you must mean Edwardo. I hope things have gone well. They've been talking for quite awhile."

Jeremy's heart sank even further. "You want them to get back together?"

Claire shook her head. "No, that's not what I meant. They just had a lot to discuss. Come to her room with us. She needs to see you." Claire linked her arms with Jeremy's and Rick's and guided the two men down the hall. Jeremy's instinctive reaction was to run in the opposite direction, but he allowed Claire to lead him anyway. He just hoped she knew what she was doing.

Claire nudged Jeremy ahead of her as they entered Candice's room. Edwardo still sat in the chair next to the bed, and Candice continued to sleep. Tension mounted between Jeremy and Edwardo, and Rick cleared his throat uncomfortably. The noise roused Candice, and she opened her eyes.

Her gaze rested on Jeremy. "Hi, Jeremy. You're here," she said softly. The mere effort required to speak seemed too much, and she closed her eyes again.

Jeremy forgot about Edwardo and Candice's family as he approached the bed. He couldn't take his gaze from that precious face. A wide white bandage covered her temple, and dark circles ringed her eyes, but she had never looked more beautiful to him. "Of course I'm here."

A soft smiled played on her lips. "Pull a chair closer and sit by my bed," she instructed without opening her eyes. "I don't want to shout. My head hurts."

Edwardo rose and offered his chair. He didn't appear pleased, but he graciously moved out of the way. "I'm going now, Candi," he said as he approached the bed. "I'll see you tomorrow." Edwardo bent and brushed his lips across her cheek.

"All right, Edwardo. We can talk more then," she answered with a sigh.

Jeremy was glad Edwardo was leaving. After all the damage he had done, Jeremy didn't feel comfortable around him and didn't trust him. He didn't want the man to come back and see Candice ever again.

"I've missed you, Jeremy. I'm so glad you're here," Candice said.

Jeremy pulled his chair closer to the bed so he wouldn't have to strain to hear. Candice spoke so softly that he knew she was in much discomfort.

"What were you doing on that snowmobile with Edwardo?" Jeremy asked, unable to resist knowing the whole truth, yet afraid to hear it.

"It was a terrible accident, but I don't want to talk about that, Jeremy. Let's talk about your work. Have you got the windows in yet? Can you start working on the next unit?"

"Almost. We have a few things left before the final walk-through. It has come together nicely."

"I'm glad, Jeremy. I was so afraid you hated me for what Edwardo did. I've been so lonely for you." Candice's words were getting slower and softer as she spoke.

"I could never hate you, Candice, and I never blamed you. Don't ever think that." Jeremy reached out and touched her fingers that stuck out from the cast. She curled her fingers around his.

"I have something to tell you Jeremy, and it's really important. . .but I'm so sleepy. Can I tell you tomorrow?"

Before Jeremy could answer, Candice had already drifted back to sleep. Claire gave him a sympathetic smile.

"It's the pain medicine they've given her. She can't stay awake for too long. She never did handle medication well. If it makes most people drowsy, it'll knock Candi out for hours."

Jeremy nodded but didn't answer. He knew he wouldn't leave until he'd heard what Candice wanted to tell him.

ᴥ

Candice opened her eyes in the dimly lit room. She knew she had slept for a long time because Rick and Claire were gone. She also knew it wasn't yet morning because the hustle and bustle of the morning staff had not yet started. A shaft of light cut into the dim shadows as a nurse came in through the door. Candice shifted slightly.

"Oh good, you're awake," the woman said. "I hate waking patients when I take their vitals." The nurse reached for Candice's good arm and rolled up the sleeve. "I'll just take your pressure, then you can get back to sleep," she said in a low voice.

Candice wondered why the woman was whispering until she noticed someone was asleep in the chair beside her bed.

She turned slightly, trying not to agitate her throbbing head. Jeremy was slumped in the chair with his chin low and his hands folded over his chest.

"Poor man. He doesn't look comfortable, does he?" she murmured.

The nurse glanced at Jeremy. "I couldn't get him to leave, and he refused a cot. Said he would be just fine in that chair. I told him he would be stiff in the morning, but he didn't mind." The nurse shifted topics as she checked Candice's pulse. "I hear this is your last day here."

"I get to go home?" Candice asked, brightening at the thought.

"The doctor will want to check you first. But if you're out of the woods, you'll be released."

As the nurse finished checking her patient's vitals, Candice continued to stare at Jeremy. He didn't look comfortable, but Candice was glad he'd decided to stay. Hospitals made her feel so lonely. Jeremy's presence was comforting and made her feel secure. As the nurse bustled out of the room, Jeremy shifted in his chair. Slowly he opened his eyes. It took a moment for him to realize where he was, then he stretched his arms overhead. He looked like a big yawning lion to Candice.

"You should have let them get you a cot," Candice scolded.

"Good morning to you too," Jeremy answered in a gruff voice. He cleared his throat. "How are you feeling?"

"Better, I think. Definitely sore, but I don't feel like a marching band is tromping through my head. I get to go home today."

Jeremy nodded. "That's good. But won't you need someone to help you for a while?"

"Claire said Mom and Dad are coming. They can stay at the apartment until I decide where I'm going next." She tapped the cast. "I'm definitely done skiing for the season." Candice quietly studied Jeremy's face. His face was in shadows, but that didn't matter because she had every line of his features etched in her mind. "Jeremy?"

"Mm-hmm?"

"I wanted to tell you about Edwardo."

Jeremy suddenly sat straighter in his chair, his posture belying his casual tone. "What about him?"

"He and I worked things out. He explained a lot to me, things I needed to hear. Remember how you said I needed to find out what was holding me back from fully experiencing God's grace for me? I found it, Jeremy. It was my relationship with Edwardo. Finally, I'm free."

Jeremy didn't respond, and the silence grew between them.

"Don't you understand what I'm saying, Jeremy? I'm free. I finally know what it's like to bask in the glory of God's grace."

"Are you getting back together with Edwardo? Is that what you feel has been holding you back?" Jeremy asked.

"No. I'm not explaining this very well. Jeremy, last night Edwardo explained a lot about his view of our past relationship. The things he shared were very important for me to hear because they softened my heart toward him. He asked me to forgive him. That's what has been holding me back. It was my unwillingness to forgive. Instead of dealing with my anger at him, I buried my feelings deep in my heart. I thought it was over, but those ugly emotions were festering. And when Edwardo appeared, all those ugly things burst forth. I was so angry with him that I think I hated him, and you know how God feels about hatred. So when he asked me to forgive him, and I did, it was like chains were falling away from my heart. The ice melted, and I felt so free and warm and refreshed. I actually felt the presence of my heavenly Father as He smiled upon me. I'm free, Jeremy. I'm finally free of my past, and I can move forward."

Candice could tell her words moved Jeremy. He rose slowly from his chair and moved closer to her. "I love you so much, Candice," he said hoarsely. "Please say you love me too."

"Oh, Jeremy, you shouldn't even have to ask. Of course I love you!"

❧

"You're glowing," Claire stated as she walked into the room at eight o'clock that morning. She waddled over to the chair Jeremy had slept in and sat down in a heap.

Candice nodded. "I suppose I am. I still feel pretty rough, but the sun must be shining brighter today." She gently reached for a piece of toast on her tray and took a bite. "Would you comb my hair for me? I'm sure I look frightful."

Claire raised her eyebrows. "Do you have someone to impress? I noticed the guys are lining up at your door just like they always do. And I don't know how you do it either. Both your eyes are black, yet men are still hanging all over you."

Candice rolled her eyes at her sister's sarcasm. "Please, Claire. Will you just comb my hair without any of your comments? I feel like I have a bird's nest sitting on top of my head."

Claire grabbed a brush out of her purse and approached Candice. Ever so gently she pulled it through Candice's thick blond hair. Candice winced when the brush hit a few snags.

"What do you think of Jeremy?" Candice asked.

"I like him. He sort of reminds me of Rick." Claire continued to brush Candice's hair as a companionable silence filled the air.

"Do you remember when we were kids how we both planned to marry princes? Then we would be princesses. Does Rick still call you his princess?"

Claire nodded, color filling her cheeks. "Yes, and I hope he always will."

Candice sighed. "I hope I've found my prince too."

Before Claire could answer, the door opened and Edwardo strode into the room. He carried a large bouquet of red roses. Claire groaned, but no one seemed to notice.

"You're here bright and early," Candice commented. Edwardo placed the vase on the small table near her bed.

"I have a proposal for you," he said, his voice wavering.

Candice and Claire locked gazes. "I think I'll go look for some juice. Rick says I don't get enough vitamin C." Claire made a hasty retreat.

Candice was sorry to see her sister go. She needed her sister there to keep the conversation light and manageable. "What sort of proposal, Edwardo?"

Edwardo cleared his voice nervously. "Here," he handed her the small box containing her engagement ring. Candice refused to take it, and Edwardo set the box on the tray beside Candice.

"I want us back together. I think we could pick up where we left off, don't you? Since our talk last night, I feel like we finally understand each other. We've always had a good time, and I've never felt for any woman what I feel for you. Besides, you always said we were meant for each other. What do you think?"

Candice reached for the box and pried it open. The beautiful diamond twinkled in the light. "Edwardo, I'm glad we have finally resolved the past. But that doesn't mean we have a future together. I cannot marry you, Edwardo. I love someone else." Candice braced herself for his smooth rebuttal.

Edwardo reached for the ring box and gently took it from

Candice's hand. "You don't love me anymore," he said softly as though he was just realizing the truth. "That's hard for me to accept. Maybe that's the reason I've been pushing you to come back to me." He stuffed the small box into his pocket. "Are you sure this is how you want it?"

Candice nodded firmly. "I'm sure, Edwardo. We can be friends." She studied his features. He didn't seem angry or hurt as she'd expected.

"Friends." He paused. "I don't want to just be friends. It would never be enough for me. I think it must be time to part ways." He placed a gentle kiss on Candice's forehead, then moved toward the door.

Candice was surprised yet thankful for the way he'd accepted her refusal. "May God bless you, Edwardo."

He gave her a small wave. "Don't worry about me, Candi Kiss. I'm off to conquer new mountains."

ɞ

Jeremy felt like he was walking on air. After his conversation with Candice in the early morning hours, he'd decided to find a motel room and catch a few more hours of sleep. He hadn't wanted to leave, but Candice had insisted. And she had been right: that chair was not made for sleeping. So he found a motel near the hospital. After getting a room he stretched out on the bed and daydreamed about Candice. Quickly his eyelids grew so heavy that he couldn't hold them open.

Though his sleep was deep and restful, he didn't need much. He was wide awake two hours later and ready to go. After a quick shave and shower, he was off to the hospital again. He wanted to be the one to drive Candice home. After all, she was his woman. She loved him!

As he walked through the doors of the hospital, he noticed some fresh white daisies in the florist's window. He quickly purchased them and then hurried to the elevators. He barely made it in time; the doors were closing as he reached it.

"Hold the elevator!" he called. He quickly crowded into the elevator, noticing a handsome older couple inside. "Thanks," he said as he pressed the button to the second floor.

"Those are lovely flowers," the woman said, smiling at Jeremy. "Daisies are my favorite," she added.

Jeremy returned the smile. "They are for someone very special. She told me last night that she loves me. I'm trying to find the right time to ask her to marry me," he confided.

"You seem like a kind young man. Any woman would feel blessed to have you for a husband," the woman responded.

"I'm not so sure about that," Jeremy answered, color rising in his face.

The man put his arm around his wife's shoulders as the elevator doors slid open. "Don't mind Sophie. She just loves romance. Now you do what you feel is right. God will bless you."

Jeremy nodded, thinking on the man's words. He was right. If he obeyed what was right in his heart, God would bless it. And he knew in his heart that loving Candice was right. He followed the couple out of the elevator and turned down a different hall. Clutching the flowers in front of him, he hurried to Candice's room, determined to talk with her before he lost his nerve.

As he reached the room, he took a deep breath to calm his suddenly rattled nerves, then pushed open the door. "Hi, Beautiful," he greeted as he walked into the room. She was alone, sitting up in bed. She looked more alert and comfortable than she had the night before.

Candice beamed at him. "Hi, Jeremy. Did you get enough sleep?"

"Mm-hm," Jeremy answered as he approached the hospital

bed and handed her the daisies. He noticed the bouquet of red roses out of the corner of his eye. They were sitting on the floor in the corner of the room. "It's beginning to look like a flower shop in here," he commented.

Candice gladly received the flowers. "I love daisies. They're my favorite flower. I'm so glad you brought them." She took the vase and set it on her little table right next to the bed. With a contented smile she turned back to Jeremy. "I get to go as soon as the doctor comes to check on me. Probably in the next hour."

Jeremy nodded, suddenly nervous again. "Candice, there's something I need to ask you." He swallowed the huge lump that lodged in his throat. His mouth was dry, and the words seemed to stick on his tongue.

Candice turned to him with wide eyes. "What is it? Is there something wrong?"

Gently Jeremy brushed her fingers with his own, suddenly afraid to make eye contact with her. "No, Honey, there's nothing wrong. I just need to know if you'll marry me." He looked up to find Candice staring wide-eyed at him. He wondered if he had spoken too soon. Perhaps she wasn't ready to commit herself to him right after she got things straightened out with Edwardo. Jeremy glanced at the beautiful red roses on the floor and wondered if maybe he had spoken out of turn. Edwardo may have come back and charmed his way into her graces. He let go of her hand, ready to take back the proposal if she wished.

"Okay," came Candice's soft answer.

"Okay? You mean you want to be my wife?" Jeremy asked uncertainly.

Candice nodded emphatically. "Yes, Jeremy, there's nothing I'd like more than to be your wife."

If it hadn't been for her cast and broken rib, Jeremy would

have swept her into his arms. Instead he gingerly took her chin in his hand and placed a warm kiss on her lips. "I love you," he whispered, looking into her eyes and receiving the love he found glowing from their depths.

Candice was about to answer when she noticed they weren't alone. A wide grin spread across her face. "Hi, Daddy."

Jeremy turned to find the elevator couple standing in the doorway. The woman was dabbing her eyes with a handkerchief, and the man was studying Jeremy with his arms crossed over his chest.

"I see you asked your girl to marry you. I just had no idea it would be my daughter!" the man boomed.

Before Jeremy could stammer out a reply, the man crossed the room and stuck out his hand. "Welcome to the family, Son. You must be Jeremy." Within seconds the room became crowded with Claire, Rick, and Candice's parents. Everyone began talking at once. The ladies started planning the wedding, while the men discussed where Jeremy worked and where the couple would live. Jeremy caught Candice's gaze, and all the commotion seemed to cease around them. In that secret moment they shared an unspoken message of love. Both Candice and Jeremy knew that it was God's grace that had brought them together.

epilogue

Candice and Jeremy had been married less than a month when they received a special phone call. "You just keep painting the spare bedroom while I get the phone," Candice called over her shoulder. She chuckled at Jeremy's answering grumbles.

She picked up the receiver, hoping she wouldn't get any paint smudges on it. "Hello?"

Rick was on the other end. "Candi! You're an aunt. And you're not going to believe this!"

"Twins?" Candice asked, joking.

"Yes! And they're girls!" he added with a good-natured chuckle. He quickly told Candice that their names were April and Allison; both weighed less than six pounds, and they were only an hour old. "I have to go. Claire is just fine, but I think she has her hands full."

Candice hung up the receiver and called out to her husband, "Jeremy, you are not going to believe this—"

Before she could finish telling him the news, the phone rang again. She picked up the receiver and listened to the brief message. Dazed, Candice hung up the receiver and slowly sank to the floor.

Jeremy walked into the room. Paint was splattered across his cheek and all over his clothes. "What am I not going to believe?" He walked over to Candice and knelt beside her. "Candice? Are you all right? Who was on the phone?" he asked again.

Candice shook her head and stared up at him. "Which news do you want first?"

"Well, let's start with the first call."

"Claire and Rick have twin girls: April and Allison."

Jeremy grinned. "Claire and Rick are going to be very busy parents. Now tell me the next news."

"Do you know how I've had a hard time getting over the flu?"

Jeremy nodded. "You've been sick quite a bit."

Candice swallowed hard, still absorbing the information from her doctor. "It's not the flu. We're going to have a baby too." She stared uncertainly at Jeremy. She hoped he wouldn't be disappointed that they were starting their family so soon after getting married.

Jeremy's grin spread wide across his face. "I guess we're going to be busy parents too." He gently enfolded her into his arms. "I love you, Candice, my sweet little penguin," he whispered against her forehead. "I'm so glad you are my wife, and I'm also excited about the baby."

Candice nodded, overcome with emotion. "I love you too," she answered. She couldn't believe how gracious God had been to her. He had forgiven her for so much and had never stopped loving her. Her heart took wings and flew to her heavenly Father's arms. "God's grace is so good," she whispered in awe.

Jeremy nodded. "Amen and amen."

A Letter To Our Readers

Dear Reader:

In order that we might better contribute to your reading enjoyment, we would appreciate your taking a few minutes to respond to the following questions. We welcome your comments and read each form and letter we receive. When completed, please return to the following:

Rebecca Germany, Fiction Editor
Heartsong Presents
PO Box 719
Uhrichsville, Ohio 44683

1. Did you enjoy reading *Extreme Grace* by Tish Davis?
   ☐ Very much! I would like to see more books
      by this author!
   ☐ Moderately. I would have enjoyed it more if

   _____

   _____

   _____

2. Are you a member of **Heartsong Presents**? Yes ☐ No ☐
   If no, where did you purchase this book?_____

   _____

3. How would you rate, on a scale from 1 (poor) to 5 (superior), the cover design?_____

4. On a scale from 1 (poor) to 10 (superior), please rate the following clements.

   _____ Heroine   _____ Plot

   _____ Hero   _____ Inspirational theme

   _____ Setting   _____ Secondary characters

5. These characters were special because_____

_____

_____

6. How has this book inspired your life?_____

_____

_____

7. What settings would you like to see covered in future
   Heartsong Presents books?_____

_____

_____

8. What are some inspirational themes you would like to see
   treated in future books?_____

_____

_____

9. Would you be interested in reading other **Heartsong
   Presents** titles?   Yes ☐   No ☐

10. Please check your age range:
    ☐ Under 18   ☐ 18-24   ☐ 25-34
    ☐ 35-45   ☐ 46-55   ☐ Over 55

Name _____

Occupation _____

Address _____

City _____ State _____ Zip _____

Email _____

·······Presents·······

Great Inspirational Romance at a Great Price!

Heartsong Presents books are inspirational romances in contemporary and historical settings, designed to give you an enjoyable, spirit-lifting reading experience. You can choose wonderfully written titles from some of today's best authors like Hannah Alexander, Irene B. Brand, Yvonne Lehman, Tracie Peterson, and many others.

When ordering quantities less than twelve, above titles are $2.95 each.
Not all titles may be available at time of order.

Hearts♥ng Presents
Love Stories Are Rated G!

That's for godly, gratifying, and of course, great! If you love a thrilling love story but don't appreciate the sordidness of some popular paperback romances, **Heartsong Presents** is for you. In fact, **Heartsong Presents** is the *only inspirational romance book club* featuring love stories where Christian faith is the primary ingredient in a marriage relationship.

Sign up today to receive your first set of four never-before-published Christian romances. Send no money now; you will receive a bill with the first shipment. You may cancel at any time without obligation, and if you aren't completely satisfied with any selection, you may return the books for an immediate refund!

Imagine. . .four new romances every four weeks—two historical, two contemporary—with men and women like you who long to meet the one God has chosen as the love of their lives. . .all for the low price of $9.97 postpaid.

To join, simply complete the coupon below and mail to the address provided. **Heartsong Presents** romances are rated G for another reason: They'll arrive *Godspeed!*